ALL in the FAMILY

Stories that
hit home

ALL in the FAMILY

Stories that hit home

Edited by **Tony Bradman**

A & C Black • London

First published 2008 by
A & C Black Publishers Ltd
38 Soho Square, London, W1D 3HB

www.acblack.com

Collection copyright © 2008 Tony Bradman
Stories copyright © 2008 Karen Ball, Kim Kitson, Jo Nadin,
Linda Newbery, Helen Williams, Tim Wynne-Jones

The right of Tony Bradman to to be identified as the
editor of this work has been asserted by him in accordance
with the Copyrights, Designs and Patents Act 1988.

ISBN 978-0-7136-8505-3

A CIP catalogue for this book is available from the British Library.

This book is produced using paper that is made from wood
grown in managed, sustainable forests. It is natural, renewable
and recyclable. The logging and manufacturing processes conform
to the environmental regulations of the country of origin.

Printed and bound Great Britain by MPG Books Limited.

Contents

Introduction *by Tony Bradman*   7

Alan *by Jo Nadin*   11

Beach Sounds *by Karen Ball*   31

Accidental Hero *by Linda Newbery*   47

Finding My Roots *by Helen Williams*   75

Christmas with Auntie Annie Ping Pong

    by Tim Wynne-Jones   99

After the Storm *by Kim Kitson*   117

About the Authors   141

Introduction
by Tony Bradman

I sometimes think it's strange how just one word can stand for so many different things. Take the word *family*, for example. What image pops into your mind when you hear it? Perhaps it's a group of four people – Mum, Dad and two kids. Quite possibly, it's a different image altogether. For like people themselves, families come in all shapes and sizes.

Divorce wasn't very common back in the 1960s, when I was a child, but my mum and dad managed to get one all the same. So I grew up in a family of three; my mum, my sister and me, with occasional visits from my dad. I remember being pretty envious of my mate Colin. His mum and dad weren't divorced, so he got to see *his* dad all the time. Still, maybe there were some disadvantages to your mum and dad being

7

together. Colin had 14 brothers and sisters. That's right – *fourteen*.

My big sister and I had our ups and downs. There was the time when she tried to blind me with hairspray, although she claims I was being irritating in the way that only a difficult little brother can be. And to be honest, we got on well most of the time (and still do). But things weren't so good in the rest of our extended family. My dad didn't get on with his brother particularly, and as for *his* mum, my granny – well, let's just say that the family feud between her and my mum went on for years.

I do remember some good times, though, and I think all those early experiences left me with an interest in families. I've always been keen to find out about other people's families – what they're like and how they feel about them. That's why I really enjoyed collecting together these stories. They come from all over the world, and show just how different families can be from each other – but also how alike they can be, too.

In Kim Kitson's beautiful *After The Storm*, an Australian boy discovers that he's part of a big family even though both his parents are dead. In Jo Nadin's very funny *Alan* another boy has to come to terms with his parents' divorce and their creation of new families. It's an accident that has changed things for ever for the family in Karen Ball's moving *Beach Sounds*. In Helen Williams's fascinating *Finding My Roots* a girl from the UK goes back to Jamaica, where her family came from originally, and finds out just how wide and deep her roots go. An incident in Linda Newbery's *Accidental Hero* helps a boy to see his parents in a new light. And in Tim Wynne-Jones's *Christmas with Auntie Annie Ping Pong* we see one of the youngest members of a family worrying about one of the oldest.

So, as you can see, that one little word does cover an awful lot. That's why we called this book *All in the Family*. And I hope you'll agree that we're all in these stories, however different our backgrounds might be.

10

Alan
by Jo Nadin

Monday

It was OK when Alan lived on Pilkington Street.
Then we only saw him when he came to pick
Mum up and Gran babysat for us and she let us
eat Sugar Puffs for tea and stay up for her soap
on telly. But now he is here all the time and
he eats all the Sugar Puffs and kisses Mum even
in the morning when his breath smells of stale
stuff and they use tongues which is disgusting
and she could catch MRSA off him. Fat Harriet
next door says she has seen an MRSA it was
green and the size of a Murray Mint. But she
also says she has met a vampire which I know
for a fact is a total lie.

Tuesday

I don't know what Mum sees in Alan. He is short

and is a nurse and reads comics even though he is 35. Plus he is vegetarian. Mum says she is thinking of becoming vegetarian, too. It is because Alan is mental and is brainwashing her like in James Bond. I asked Mum if I had to call him "Dad" when they are married. She said I could call him what I like and I said "mental Alan" and she said no. Then Mum asked us if we wanted to be double-barrelled i.e. Billy and Stan Jones-Allsop. I said not likely. Stan said yes. It's because he thinks it will make him more like Archie Palmer-Thomas who is second toughest in Year 4. Also he likes Alan because Alan gave him a complete set of Ninja Turtles off eBay but Donatello's arm fell off last Thursday. I said he should ask our dad for a better one for his birthday but Stan said Dad didn't even send him a card until two days late last year. I said it was because he was on an undercover operation for his newspaper at the time or possibly doing freelance work for MI5 like in James Bond. That is the sort of thing Dad would do. He is six foot tall. And lives in London now. I know what London is like. I have seen it on telly. Everyone lives in loft apartments, which is where everything is in one room. Except for the toilet because that would be disgusting having to see someone poo while you are watching a cookery programme for instance. I am going to go and stay there soon. Mum is checking a weekend with him when he is not too busy i.e. investigating criminals. Stan says he is not going because he will miss his cartoons, but he is mental and anyway Mum can record them.

Wednesday

The wedding is in less than three weeks i.e. on Saturday 27th when statistically it will not rain according to bbc.co.uk/weather. But anyway it will not be happening rain or no rain because I am going to PLOT HIS DOWNFALL. I have read all about it in How to Deal with Villains by Dick Dare which is about how to be a spy etc. All I need to do is to find out Alan's weaknesses and then attack. Then Mum will see he is totally hopeless and will beg Dad to come back and live here again. Or maybe we could all move to his loft apartment and have beds in the air and a fridge with orange juice in a tap.

Thursday

I have bought a book to PLOT HIS DOWNFALL in. It is a purple spiral ringbound A4 one from WHSmith. I have already got three sections. There is Plan A and Plan B. Dick Dare says it is essential to have a Plan B in case Plan A gets derailed at the last minute. Plus I have a whole page for "Weaknesses". Fat Harriet came with me to the shop after school. She bought a girl magazine and a Mars Bar. I said there were 294 calories in a Mars Bar but she said she lost half a stone last week because of getting the runs in Benidorm.

Friday

I have been working on the DOWNFALL and I already have a Plan A and Plan B. I am going to implement Plan A next week once I have sorted out the details because Dick Dare says it is all about the details. I would have done the details after school except Fat Harriet brought her new hamster over. He is golden coloured and is called Ashley and runs around the front room inside a see-through ball. But then Stan kicked the ball and Ashley spun too fast and Alan told

Stan off and I said you can't tell him off you're not our dad and Mum said no but he's a grown-up and Stan just kicked a hamster. I said it was an accident wasn't it Stan and Stan said no I just wanted to see how fast he would go. Then Harriet went home with Ashley and I went upstairs and now I am too annoyed to do Plan A.

Saturday

Mum made us get our suits for the wedding today. They are blue and shiny and have shirts and stripy ties. Stan wore his home and is watching telly in it. Mum says he has to take it off before tea in case he gets Angel Delight or spaghetti hoops down the front and it is dry clean only which costs a fortune. Mum showed us her wedding dress as well. It is white with gold bits. She said how do I look and I said whatever. So Mum asked Stan instead and he said like Princess Leah in *Star Wars*. He is obsessed with *Star Wars* mainly because Alan is. But she did look a bit like a princess I suppose. I hope Alan does not wear a Jedi outfit like he wore to Fat Harriet's mum's fancy dress party last year. Although obviously none of us will be wearing anything. Not that we will be in the nuddy. I mean that the wedding will be off. Because of the DOWNFALL.

Sunday

Fat Harriet came over today. She says she has got a new dress for the wedding it is silvery and I can dance with her at the disco afterwards if I like. I said no thanks and anyway they weren't getting married. Harriet said oh have they had a row. My mum had a row with Dave (i.e. her stepdad) about the sink last week and they didn't talk for three days. I said no it is because Mum has realised that Alan is totally wrong for her and that she is still in love with my dad. So Harriet said is that Alan on the drive with your mum. It was. They were carrying Tesco's bags and kissing. Harriet said it looks like it is all back on again, that is love for you I read about it in a magazine. Then we played Twister until teatime.

Monday

I did Plan A this morning because I saw an opportunity and seized it which is what Dick

Dare says you should do because a good plan is all about surprise. And details. But mostly surprise. Plan A was to make Alan late for work because he has to drop us off at school before going to hospital to be a nurse and he will get sacked if he is late and Mum can't take us because she is on check-in at the airport on earlies. So I ate my Sugar Puffs one puff at a time and chewed each one ten times. Alan said what's up Billy usually you wolf down the lot so quickly you make Jabba the Hut look refined and I said I am just chewing properly like you are supposed to I saw it on telly. Then Alan said well get a move on kiddo because we'll all be late and I don't want the Sister of No Mercy (i.e. ward Sister Brown who is his boss and a woman, ha) on my case again. So I said well I don't want to choke so you'll have to wait. Then Alan said are you trying to make me late. So I said yes because it was the truth so he said right you've got one minute or there will trouble. And I said what sort of trouble and he said well you'll have to walk to school on your own because me and Stan are going. And I said Stan will wait with me but Stan already had his coat on and said no I won't

I want to go in the car. This is because he was wearing his new wedding shoes to show Miss Llewellyn his teacher who is from Wales. So I said I will phone Mum at the airport and tell her you abandoned me home alone like in that film which is illegal and against the law and Alan said be my guest so I did ring Mum and she said is Alan there and I said he is waiting in the car and she said well he hasn't abandoned you has he so leave the Sugar Puffs and go to school now and stop being so flaming childish. So I did. I should have done more detail. Dick Dare would have known what to do. Tonight I am going to do the detail on Plan B. It is called the Great Sausage Swap and will work for sure because tomorrow is Tuesday and that means bangers and mash for tea.

Tuesday
What I did was I put some of our Tesco's pork sausages inside Alan's Linda McCartney sausages box and threw the real Linda McCartney ones away. So Mum cooked just real sausages but in two separate frying pans because Alan doesn't like meat fat on his food.

Mum said it's amazing how realistic those Linda McCartney's are I don't think I'll miss meat at all if I give it up and I thought that's what you think and Alan said are you sure these are Linda's and Mum said of course what do you think I'm trying to do poison you. Chance would be a fine thing. And I said are you enjoying your bangers and mash Alan and Alan said why thank you young Billy yes I am and Stan said those aren't Linda's those are real ones look there's some gristle and Alan went pale and then ran to the loo and spat the sausage out and Mum went after him and I could hear her saying sorry Alan and he said didn't you check and she said they were definitely in the Linda box. And then she went quiet and came back in and said Billy Jones did you swap the sausages over so that Alan ate meat and I said why doesn't Alan eat meat it's not normal and she said that's not for you to decide now go to your room Stan can have your mousse. Which was not what was supposed to happen. In Plan B Alan was supposed to shout at her and Mum would say well you are stupid for being a vegetarian and then Alan would move back to Pilkington Street. So now I need a Plan

C. Dick Dare did not mention a Plan C.

Wednesday

Mum said she had got some news for me after school. I said what is it are you pregnant like Fat Harriet's mum was. She said no she had talked to Dad and I can go and stay on Saturday for one whole night in London. So now I have my Plan C I am going to move in with Dad in London and go to school there and Mum and Stan will come too in the end and Alan will stay behind here. I have written it all in my DOWNFALL book.

Friday

Tomorrow I am going to live with my real dad. Mum asked if I was worried and I said why would I be worried he was my real dad and she said well you haven't seen him since he moved six months ago and I said well me and Stan get a letter every month and she said I know Billy but what I mean is you've never stayed on your own anywhere before and I said I'm not going to be on my own I'm going to be with my real dad so Mum rolled her eyes and I went upstairs to pack my worldly belongings. I have used our big suitcase from Cornwall last year because I need the space. I am taking all my clothes including my school uniform, football kit and swimming trunks plus three tubes of toothpaste, my maths textbook and all my Harry Potters. Mum said that's a big bag Billy you're only going for one night and I said whatever because if I told her the truth she would turn evil and not let me go and part of Plan C is that she has to see Dad tomorrow being tall and spy-like at his loft apartment and she will be in love with him again and we can all stay and Alan can drive home on his own and move back to Pilkington Street.

Saturday

Dad does not live in a loft apartment it is 12 Elm Road in Lewisham. When Alan stopped outside I said he had got it wrong Dad lives in that big tower over there and Alan said what Canary Wharf and mum looked at me all funny like she looked at us when our rabbit Elvis died. And I said well he does. And she said welcome to the real world Billy and I said I was in the real world I wasn't living in the 13th dimension or anything like on Stan's cartoons. Then Dad opened the door and said all right Billy boy. He is not as tall as I remember but he is definitely bigger than Alan. I thought he and Alan might get into a fight over Mum then and there and Alan would be left battered in the multicoloured gravel but they just talked about football and whether Palace were going to beat Sunderland tomorrow. Dad said where's Stan and Mum said he was with Granny and maybe he would come next time and Dad said whenever he's ready. Then Mum said we'll pick him up at 11 tomorrow and Dad said OK and then they drove off. Dad said give us your bag Billy blimey what have you got in here everything but the kitchen sink and I said Dick Dare says it is best to be prepared for any eventuality. So Dad said well he is right whoever he is. Then we went in and he said welcome to Jones Towers son it's not a mansion but it's home. He is right it is not a mansion. There is no wallpaper in the hall just bare walls and no carpet either. But it's probably a cover and he really does live in a loft and he is just here while he keeps an eye on some terrorists over the road or something. Then Dad showed me my room. It is the smallest bedroom out of two and has yellow duck wallpaper which is a bit babyish but we can repaint it soon. I unpacked everything and hung my school uniform up properly because it is important to make a good impression on your first day at a new school. Then Dad came back in and said he would order pizza for tea and what did I like and I said what do you like and he said American Hot and I said that is what I like too because we are genetic but Alan likes vegetarian feast.

But then we were eating American Hot and watching Sky and the doorbell went and it was a woman with shiny black hair and a big tummy and dad said Billy I'd like you to meet my girlfriend Frances. And she said hello Billy I've heard all about you but I pretended I hadn't heard her and carried on watching Sky until she said I'll go and make some tea shall I and Dad said thanks sweetheart.

And I said why is she so fat she's like Fat Harriet's mum and Dad said Billy I've got something to tell you me and Frances are having a baby isn't that amazing you are going to have a new baby brother or sister and I said oh. Then we didn't say anything for a bit and then I said but it won't be my brother or sister because Frances isn't my mum. And then Dad said why have you got all your school uniform here Billy and I said because I'm coming to live here with you and I can go to the school down the road that I saw when Mum dropped me off and we can watch Palace at weekends. But Dad said oh Billy boy you know I can't have you here with me there'll be no room once Frances moves in and I said but I thought it was my bedroom and Dad said no Billy that room is for the baby we've just done it up. So I said I could sleep right here on the sofa and Dad said but Billy I work nights at the paper and I said is that because you are working undercover in the field and he said no because that is when I have to check the computers are all working when the paper goes to print and I said is that a cover because you can't tell me you are really a spy and he said no Billy it is the truth. Then he said son you've got a home and your mum and Alan love you and I said I don't love Alan and Dad said I know it's hard but he's a good bloke and I said he reads comics and dad said well that's grand you can borrow them off him instead of spending your own pocket money. And then Frances came in with the tea and Dad said are you all right Billy why don't you watch telly with us and I said no I'd rather go to bed now thanks and so I did because Dick Dare says never expose your weaknesses. Anyway Dad is still a spy. I mean a real spy wouldn't admit to it not even to his own son so he is definitely still a spy.

Sunday

Frances was still here when I got up and she kissed Dad with tongues while he made toast and Marmite. I said Fat Harriet says you can catch MRSA like that and they're the size of Murray Mints and green, but Frances laughed and said if they were the size of Murray Mints I'd be on the wards with a net and Dad said Frances is a nurse Billy. And I said it is a coincidence that she and Alan are nurses only Dick Dare says there are no coincidences only conspiracies and Dad said yes we are all conspiring to make sure you are healthy and he and Frances laughed and

I laughed inside but not outside because I don't want to reveal a weakness. Then I said have you ever seen a man with only one ear because a dog bit it off because Alan has he had to put the ear in the fridge until a man sewed it back. And Frances said that sounds amazing, but I work in the geriatric ward helping old people it is quite fascinating and Dad said and stressful and she said yes. And I said that's what Alan says. Then we watched Sky until 11.

When Mum and Alan came to pick me up Frances came to say hello and I said Frances is a nurse it is a conspiracy and Alan said yes we're conspiring to make you healthy and I laughed on the outside because I forgot about revealing a weakness and that I hate Alan. Dad said how is Stan and Mum says he was fine but he had broken Granny's china cat and that maybe both of us could come for a day in the holidays and Dad says yes we'd like that wouldn't we Frances. Then there was cheering on the telly and Dad ran inside and it was 1-0 to Palace and Alan said nice one. And Mum rolled her eyes at Frances and said men and Frances said tell me about it.

And I said can we go now please. And Dad said see you in a month or so son good luck with the wedding Lizzie and Mum said thanks and touched Alan on the arm and Alan said good luck with the baby mate. When we got in the car Mum said did you have a nice time and I said yes thanks. Mum said so you didn't try to move in then and I said no because there is no wallpaper or carpet and anyway Dad is on nights and it would interfere with him being a spy and everything. And Mum smiled and said OK Billy I'm glad and Alan said me too. And actually I was a bit glad because babies cry all the time and sometimes wee right across the room according to Fat Harriet.

Monday

Mum has been crying. It is because she has read the DOWNFALL book. I hid it under my bed but she found it when she was looking for Stan's red pants. I said are you angry but she said no Billy I am just very disappointed. Then I felt bad because I don't like it when Mum cries her eyes go red and black stuff goes down her face and she doesn't look like Princess Leah any more.

Tuesday

Fat Harriet came over after school and we played Nintendo in my bedroom. I said why don't you live with your real dad and she said I don't know I just don't so I said but don't you mind that Dave is not genetic and she said no because he can cook bacon and eggs in a smiley face and plus I get two lots of pocket money and two lots of Christmas and birthday presents. She said financially it is a good move to have two dads. I said I suppose so.

Wednesday

I told Mum I was sorry for the DOWNFALL book. Mum said that's OK Billy I just want all of us to be happy and I said but Dad is still my dad and she said of course he is.

Saturday

It was the wedding today. Stan ate three lots of trifle and was sick and Granny had to take him home but I stayed until 9 and danced with Mum and Fat Harriet. Alan didn't wear a Jedi outfit he had a suit on just like me and Stan only bigger. Dad and Frances sent a card it had a picture of a bride and groom on the front and said to Alan, Lizzie, Billy and Stan Jones-Allsop. Mum said I didn't have to be double-barrelled but I said I didn't mind if it made her happy and she said it did. But I said there is no way I am calling him Dad. He is Alan. Not mental Alan though. Just Alan. She said that's a start.

Beach Sounds
by Karen Ball

The sky was the same violet blue as the flowers that grew at the bottom of our garden. Star-shaped flowers, with five pointed petals. I floated on my back, concentrating on not moving my limbs, letting my body bob up and down with the waves. Seawater filled my ears and smudged out all the noises of the beach. It was just me and that blue sky.

"Hannah!"

I took a deep breath and kicked out with my legs, flipping over on to my belly to gaze towards the beach. My sister was waving at me and I waved back. I let my legs drift down until my toes played in the sand.

I watched Alice run after my dad, her long, blonde pigtail bouncing off her brown back. Dad was already standing at the mouth of one of the caves in the side of the cliff. He was balancing on a large, round rock that shone slippery-golden in the sunlight. Alice and my dad loved exploring the caves together. They were littered with rock pools. I didn't like the caves one bit. All those sharp edges and jumping from rock to rock. I hadn't been born into a body that wanted to go exploring. What was wrong with floating in the sea?

I scanned the crowd on the beach. I could see loads of mums – they were sharing out sandwiches, or rubbing sun lotion into their kids' skin, or waving to someone. Always keeping watch. That's what mums do. I looked for my mum. I must have drifted a bit, because it took a few seconds to spot her.

There she was. Parked in front of the ice-cream van. Our red-and-blue blanket was spread out on the sand and the cool box stood next to it. The sun glinted off the chrome wheels of the wheelchair as she sat watching – like all the other mums. Though not like all the other mums at all.

I walked out of the sea. The scars on my legs weren't so bad these days. They were a milky-white instead of the angry red they had been after the accident. I ran up the beach and threw myself on the ground.

"Oh, Hannah, you'll have sand stuck all over you now. Get on to the blanket."

I crawled forwards like a dog and collapsed. I gazed up at the sky, past Mum's head. It was still the same violet blue, with one or two tiny clouds drifting past.

"Hannah!" Dad called out. "Can you bring us a bucket and spade?"

I looked up at my mum. "They're trying to get me to join in," I said.

Mum laughed as Dad waved both his arms over his head and then nearly lost his balance.

"Well, go on then," she said. "You don't have to stay here with me. I'll be fine."

I didn't *have* to stick close to my mum. But I wanted to. I needed to.

"They won't wait for ever," Mum said. She tried to reach down to pass me the bucket and spade, but they were too far away.

I noticed a girl, about my age, watching closely as Mum's fingers played with the air, just beyond the bucket's handle. I jumped up and grabbed the stupid plastic bucket.

"Back in a bit!" I said, and ran past the girl, making sure to kick sand at her with my heels.

I picked my way across the rocks towards Dad, wishing that I'd remembered to put on my Crocs. Every rock seemed set on hurting my feet.

"Here you are," I said.

"Do you want to come with us?" he asked, peering towards the mouth of the cave. "We think we've found some crabs." His face flushed red with excitement.

"I have to get back to Mum," I said.

Dad's face clouded for an instant. "She'll be fine on her own," he said, then he looked over his shoulder at Alice.

I started to turn away, wobbling on a shiny, flat rock.

"Are you sure you don't want to come? This cave's great," Dad persisted. He was using a hand to shield his eyes from the sun and now it wasn't so easy to see his expression. But I could guess. He'd be looking concerned. Behind him, Alice was waiting with a blow-up rubber ring around her waist. Her pink swimsuit was dripping sea water.

"Come on!" she called.

Unlike a lot of my friends, I actually like my little sister. But it's been ages since we did something together, just the two of us. I think we've forgotten how. What with me sticking close to Mum and Alice keeping an eye on Dad, it doesn't leave much time for us to be sisters.

I watched Dad and Alice start to climb into the cave, along with loads of other dads and their children. It was easy to be happy if a crab in a bucket made you happy. As I stood on my shiny, wet slab of rock, my dad looked round for a final time. He beckoned to me, batting his hand through the air. *Follow me*! his hand said.

I looked back at Mum on the beach. I bit my lip until it hurt. She'd be OK for a few minutes, wouldn't she? I started to make my way over towards my dad, bending down so that I could use my hands to help me balance. I was crawling like a girl-spider over the rocks, and a laugh echoed off the rocks, up towards the blue sky.

I realised it was me laughing.

A black-and-white collie dog splashed through the water past me. I hadn't seen him coming and his bark was so loud that I jumped.

I mean, all of me jumped. Every single cell in my body jerked and suddenly I wasn't a girl-spider any more. I was just a stupid girl sat on her bottom in a rock pool, with an angry-red graze on her thigh.

I climbed back to my feet and tried to ignore the tight feeling in my chest. Dad had started to pick his way across the rocks to me.

"I'm going back to Mum," I called out, my voice shaky. I turned to the beach, and Dad didn't try to stop me.

The girl on the blanket next to us was crying, still rubbing the sand out of her face. Her mum was comforting her. My mum was staring at me, her face serious. I could see how dark her eyes were ages before I got back to the blanket.

"What?" I asked guiltily.

She shook her head. Mum was good like that – good at making me feel bad without having to say a single word. I watched her rub her legs.

The accident happened a year ago. Alice and Dad had been at home and Mum was collecting me from my dance class. I'd seen the motorcyclist and tried to call out – tried to warn her – but I'd been too late. Mum pulled down hard on the steering wheel and after that it's one big, black space. All I can remember is that I hadn't managed to warn Mum in time. If I'd called out a second earlier, things might've been different. But I hadn't. I'd been too slow and too late, and now my mum was in a wheelchair. Too bad. But I was never going to make that mistake again. I was going to look after my mum. And Alice was going to make sure nothing like that ever happened to Dad. Alice and I hadn't officially agreed all this. But we both knew. This was what we had to do from now on.

I gazed out across the sand. The tide was coming in and small crests of foam played on the waves. It was so pretty.

"Would you like to go down to the sea?" I asked Mum.

She snorted. It had been enough of an effort getting her on to the beach and had involved two strong lifeguards and a lot of people staring. Her wheelchair really dragged in the sand. "Like running through treacle," Mum had joked, trying to make me smile. But I thought that was a pretty bad joke, seeing as Mum would not be doing any running ever again. That's what the hospital had told us. The same night they'd said I was lucky not to be more seriously injured. I'd been knocked out and my legs were pretty cut up. But other than that... The doctors tried to make me feel better by telling me the odds of getting out of that car with no broken bones was one squillion to one. I felt like asking them about what odds they'd put on Mum walking again. Being in hospital was a big wake-up call. Lesson number one – life is not fair.

Thinking about all this made me angry. Looking at that other girl with her mum made me even more angry. I stomped across the sand and grabbed the rubber handles of my mum's wheelchair and started to manoeuvre it round. I felt my heart beating loudly in my chest. I wanted to burst into tears, except we already had one crybaby on the beach and I wasn't going to join her.

"Come on," I said, pulling on my sunhat. "We're going for a paddle."

Mum laughed. "You sound very serious about this," she said, reaching out to give my hand a squeeze. "OK. If that's what you want."

I pushed the wheelchair, but it wouldn't budge. A couple of lifeguards could see what I was trying to do and came over to lift my mum and her wheelchair on to the wooden walkway. Mum's face blushed pink and she couldn't stop smiling. I think she enjoyed the attention from these two big men.

"I'll be OK from here, thanks," I said, barging in front of them and taking the handles. I started to push. I knew people were watching but I blanked it out of my head. It was just me, Mum and the sea. That was all that mattered. I pushed the wheelchair along the wooden slats. Mum bounced slightly in her seat as we jerked over them. The sun shone on my bright-red sunhat and I could hear myself panting as I leaned all my weight into the wheelchair.

A boy started walking beside me. He had golden freckles scattered across the bridge of his nose and a chunk was missing from his front tooth. I pointed to my own front tooth.

"What happened?" I asked.

The boy grinned. "Cricket accident. I'm lucky to be alive."

I heard my mum start to laugh and then

struggle to turn it into a cough. I worked hard at keeping my face straight.

The boy pointed to one of the handles on the wheelchair. "Want some help?" he asked.

I took one handle and let him take the other. It was tough going, but between us, we got some speed up. Finally, we arrived at the water's edge. I went to the front of Mum's chair and let down the foot rests so that she could dangle her feet in the water. Of course, she wouldn't be able to feel the water, but that wasn't the point. My mum had come to the beach and she was going to paddle. With me keeping an eye on her, she'd be fine.

"How is it?" I asked.

Mum smiled weakly. "It's great," she said, staring out to the horizon. She didn't seem to be enjoying it as much as I wanted her to.

The boy had a bright-green Frisbee tucked under his arm. His shoulder blades stood out at sharp angles as he felt the Frisbee's weight.

"Fancy a game?" he asked, looking at Mum and me.

"I don't know..." I said.

"Yes," Mum put in quickly.

"Game on!" the boy called out, running a distance away for the first throw. I hadn't even found out what his name was. He threw the Frisbee towards me. It arced smoothly through the sky and curved round, following its invisible course. It was a good throw. I started to run through the water, racing to catch the flying disc. I leapt into the air, twisting at the waist to reach the bright-green plastic. Yes! My hands closed around it and I fell back to the beach, my toes gripping the wet sand. It felt good.

I looked round at my mum. She clapped her hands together.

"Come on!" she called. I hesitated. "Hannah! Get with it!"

I curled my hand around the edge of the Frisbee and started moving it backwards and forwards from the centre of my chest. I wasn't sure how hard to throw it. I didn't want the Frisbee to fly over Mum's head and I didn't want it to land pathetically in the water at her feet. I wanted my mum to catch it.

I launched the Frisbee into the air. The boy gave a whistle of encouragement as it soared through the sky, green against the blue. I held my breath and watched. Nothing could stop it and nothing could slow it down. It was free. I felt a lump form in my throat. I looked over at my mum. She couldn't take her eyes off it.

Then it started to fall. It seemed to take for ever. It sailed towards my mum's left shoulder. She reached out a hand, craning over the side of the wheelchair. "Woo-hoo!" she screeched.

I let go of my breath and let it hiss between my teeth. Mum was laughing, waving the Frisbee above her head. She'd caught it!

"Your mum rocks!" called out the boy, waving both hands above his head. "To me!"

I watched as Mum pulled the Frisbee back behind her head, then leant low in the wheelchair and sent the green, plastic disc in a smooth, low journey over the surface of the sea. The boy caught it easily.

"Nice throw," said a voice. I looked round. Dad was standing there, holding Alice's hand. Behind him, the boy was running back up the beach, towards a woman who was waving to him.

I walked over to my mum, dad and sister.

"There's only one small problem..." Dad looked past me.

I followed the direction of his gaze. Slowly, the wheels of my mum's wheelchair were sinking into the soft, wet sand. She was getting stuck.

Dad walked over and put a hand on my shoulder. "Come on. We need to get your mum back up the beach."

He tried to heave the wheelchair out of the water, but it wouldn't budge. "Lift me out and carry me," Mum said.

Dad walked round to the front of the wheelchair. The sun was starting to dip over the horizon and a sudden breeze made the hairs on my arms stand up. Alice came to stand close by me and I put an arm around her skinny shoulders.

We watched.

Mum smiled as Dad brought his face close to hers. I knew that Alice and I could have been on the other side of the world right then, for all they knew. It didn't feel bad to be left out; in fact, they were getting on pretty well without us. Dad reached one hand round Mum's waist and another under her legs and he lifted her out of the wheelchair. They looked like Romeo and Juliet. It was dead romantic as we watched Dad carry Mum back up the beach. You wouldn't even have known there was anything wrong with Mum's legs. And now I didn't hate all the people who were watching. Who wouldn't want to watch? I felt proud.

Alice and I turned back round to look at the wheelchair, sat there all on its own, stuck in the sand. I almost felt sorry for it.

"Want to help?" I asked my little sister.

"Sure thing," she said, running round to grab one of the handles. Alice tugged and heaved, yanked and pushed. So did I. The wheelchair wouldn't shift.

"Come on, you weakling!" my sister teased. It felt good to have her make fun of me. More fun was definitely what we needed.

"I'm trying my best!" I panted, as I gave the wheelchair an almighty shove. I used all my strength. The chair definitely moved at least two centimetres. We both collapsed over the chair, laughing. Dad walked back down the beach with the lifeguards. He'd left Mum on the blanket, sitting against the cool box. I could see her laughing and shaking her head as she watched us.

"Come on, you two," he said, as the lifeguards pushed the wheelchair back up the beach. "It's time to go."

That evening, I did something I hadn't done for years. I sat on my mum's lap. I didn't care if someone turned round to look at the pretty woman in the wheelchair. I didn't even care if someone stared at the girl with scars on her legs, who was too old for sitting on laps. I'd left caring back at the beach.

All four of us ate chips straight from the paper outside the fish and chip shop.

"Can't beat a good day out," my dad said, popping a steaming piece of battered cod into his mouth. The smell of vinegar made my nostrils flare.

Other families walked past, looking happy. The whole town seemed happy, as the promenade lights flickered on, red and green and yellow. I wasn't floating out at sea any more, all on my own. I was surrounded by the noise of other people – and it felt good.

I turned to look at my mum. "Did you have a good time today?" I asked.

"Yes, I did," she said, wiping a smear of tomato ketchup from my face.

"Thanks to you," said Dad, putting a hand on my shoulder.

I felt myself blush. They weren't about to get all emotional on me, were they?

"Well, you're my..." my voice trailed away.

"Family?" said Dad, finishing my sentence for me. He screwed up his chip paper and lobbed it into a bin.

"Something like that," I mumbled. We were something like a family.

Alice and I ran ahead to the car. Dad followed, pushing Mum in her wheelchair. I could hear the two of them talking quietly to each other.

The light was fading as our car pulled out of town. I could feel my eyelids getting heavy and Alice sagged against my side, already dozing. Since the accident, I didn't normally let myself fall asleep in the car. But today, I thought it would be OK.

The sounds of the beach faded behind us. We were going home.

Accidental Hero
by Linda Newbery

It was borrowing, not stealing. Anyone would agree, even the police, if they came after him. Not that they would.

Owen Davies was telling himself this as he rode up the track, climbing the shoulder of hillside that soon left the village below, huddled in autumn trees.

It was Mum and Dad's fault. They hadn't meant to, but they'd driven him out of the house. The way they argued, till the air seemed spiked with icicles – it made him so tight inside, so coiled, so knotted up, that he had to get away. He'd been *desperate* to get away.

It was the Bed-and-Breakfast visitor who'd started it, this time. The girl hadn't booked, just turned up on the doorstep; she'd seen the B&B sign outside, and VACANCIES in the window. It was quite late, getting on for nine. The clocks had just gone back for winter and already it seemed to have been dark for hours.

Mum wrote her name, Simpson, in the guest book; then said, "Owen, help Miss Simpson with her bags."

"Nicole," said the girl. "I haven't got a bag." She was carrying a small, black rucksack.

"You might get a meal at The Anchor, but it's a bit late," Mum said doubtfully; but Nicole Simpson replied that she wasn't hungry and was going straight to bed.

There was something wrong with her; anyone could see that. Her eyes were red, her nose sniffy. She looked barely old enough to drive, though she'd come in a red Fiesta, which was parked behind Dad's van in the lane. Mum's policy with guests was not to seem nosy. "Their private business is none of mine," was how she put it. "Long as they pay up, that's all I want."

Neither Dad nor Owen liked having the guests; it felt like being invaded. Mum fussed about keeping the bathroom clean, and not using all the hot water or having the TV too loud. That night, though, Owen wouldn't have known there was anyone staying. Nicole Simpson refused the tea and biscuits Mum offered, went to her room and stayed there. Owen heard the toilet flush; after that, not a sound.

In the morning, he sniffed hungrily while Mum fried mushrooms, eggs and bacon. She'd been caught out before when guests turned out to be vegetarian or only wanted muesli, but they were the exceptions. Full English Breakfast – not Welsh, though they were on the Welsh side of the border – was what Mum did. Breakfast for the family was cereal and toast, with FEB (as they called it) only on Sundays, or when Mum had eggs and bacon to use up.

There was no sign of Nicole Simpson.

"Give her a shout, will you?" Mum put the plate of food under the grill to keep warm.

Owen went along to the spare room, knocked, knocked again. No answer. No TV on inside, no one moving about. He opened the door enough to see that the curtains were pulled back and the bed roughly made; then opened it wide: the room was empty. No rucksack, no girl, nothing.

She'd done a bunk. Owen checked outside – the red Fiesta was gone.

"*Damn*!" Mum, hearing the news, snatched the hot plate and plonked it on the table. "You might as well have this."

Before she could change her mind, Owen sat at the place laid for the runaway, and grabbed the HP sauce. Cornflakes and toast had been over an hour ago.

"Can't you make them pay when they get here, 'stead of in the morning?" he asked, through a delicious, bacony mouthful.

"It's not how things are done."

"Why not?"

"It just isn't."

"What's up?" Dad, on his way from storeroom to shop, sensed the irritable atmosphere.

"Sneaked off without paying, that young madam! Should have guessed. One look at her—" Mum squirted washing-up liquid into the sink and plunged the frying-pan in.

"Don't know why you bother," Dad said, predictably. "More trouble than it's worth."

"You *know* why! We've got to live on *some*thing! When the shop folds, then what?"

Owen winced. Did she *want* to put Dad in a foul mood? It had been Dad's dream, running a village Post Office shop. Now he did run one; but there was nothing but worry about the future.

"That's right, put the boot in!" Dad snapped back.

And they were off.

"No one's blaming you!" Mum retaliated. "But the shop's struggling, you know it—"

"So what can I do? Set up roadblocks, stop people going to Tesco's and Sainsbury's, hijack their deliveries? Can I work any harder?"

"I'm just *saying* – if it folds, then what? Where'll you find work, round here?"

Dad's mouth shut in an obstinate line. Next thing, Mum would go *We should have stayed in Liverpool*. Might as well jab Dad in the ribs with a sharp stick. Owen chomped bacon, pretending he couldn't hear.

"Twenty pounds I won't be getting," Mum grumped, instead of using the Liverpool goad. "Can't win, can I? If I did nothing, I'd be spending money we haven't got. If I make an effort, *that's* wrong—"

"For God's *sake*! Give it a rest!" Dad went out, slamming the door hard. Mum turned up the radio, and went back to furious washing-up.

Fried egg clogged Owen's throat like a sob trying to get out. He hated it when they were like this – more and more, lately. Money, always money. Sometimes he felt guilty for taking his pocket money, for having to be fed, or needing new school shoes.

"Well! Not the best start. What're you doing today?" Mum asked, fake-cheerful.

"Dunno." Owen took his plate to the sink. Get out of here, was all he could think. Get away from *them*, and the cage they'd built around themselves.

He was in the lane, kicking at stones, when the idea came to him. Irresistible, once it was lodged in his mind.

Up on the slope behind Marches House he could see Tansy, Victoria Gamble's grey pony. Victoria was OK, but Owen had heard customers in the shop gossiping enviously about her parents. Marches House was the smartest in the village, set well back from the road, with a gravelled driveway and double garage, and a paddock behind. The Gambles had recently moved from Chester, bringing Victoria's pony, their BMW, their Range Rover and trailer. Mrs Hughes, the postman's sister, cleaned for them twice a week. "You should see it! Like one of those houses in glossy magazines," she'd told Mum; "everything just so." All that luxury, and the Gambles were hardly there to appreciate it: Victoria was a weekly boarder at some posh girls' school, and her parents worked in Chester.

It was half term now, and they'd gone to the Canary Islands, leaving the pony to the care of a girl who cycled over twice daily from the next village. I could've done that, Owen thought: grooming and feeding, and cleaning out the stable. A bit of extra pocket money would've been handy.

Tansy must be as bored as he was, in the small paddock by herself. Sometimes, when her mum wasn't around, Victoria let Owen ride. The pony had cost thousands, and had won prizes at shows; Mrs Gamble would think her far too good for Owen, who'd never had a riding lesson in his life. But Victoria liked sharing.

Why not take Tansy out now – ride up to the hills?

At once he knew he'd do it. *That* would get him away from Mum and Dad and home – miles away! The saddle and bridle were in the store beside the stable. It had looked complicated when Victoria put them on the pony, but he thought he could remember how.

Tansy came over, expecting a sugar lump or a carrot; she nudged at his pockets. Owen liked the warm, animal smell of her, and her grassy breath.

It was nice here. The Gambles' paddock had a mass of thorn trees alongside it, by a stream; the hill rose steep and brackeny beyond. The grey, louring cloud gave lushness to the grass and a coppery glow to the leaves.

Owen thought of the days out he used to have with Mum and Dad, before they'd left Liverpool. They used to drive out to North Wales, sometimes for a whole weekend. They'd take the Snowdon railway, or scramble up beside a waterfall. Mum and Dad loved the scenery so much that they'd wanted to live here – but now that they did, they hardly ever went out. Spent all hours in the shop and the storeroom, or frowning over their accounts. It was such a *waste*.

Owen's hands trembled as he opened the stable door. The saddle was on its rack, the bridle hanging beneath. He'd put everything back in place afterwards. No one need know.

Tansy was wearing her green, waterproof rug, with all sorts of buckles and hooks to hold it in place. He got that off her, then folded and stowed it inside. Sliding the bit into her mouth was the hardest part, then remembering how all the different straps fastened. But he managed it, and the pony stood quietly while he put the saddle on, remembering to tighten the girth, the way Victoria had shown him. Now he was ready.

He led the pony out through the gate and used the fence to give himself a leg-up. He put his feet in the stirrups, gathered the reins, and clicked with his tongue. Tansy moved forwards obediently.

He steered her towards the little bridge over the stream, and on up the stony track. His spirits lifted with a sense of freedom, his frustration dropping away like a shed skin. Now there was just him and Tansy, and the track leading up into the hills, and the grey, tousled sky. The pony's neck arched in front of him; her ears were pricked alertly; her hooves trod the stony path. He could pretend he was going to ride on and on, as far as the sea, and along the beach, towards Anglesey. Find her a stable for the night and ride on again the next day...

Nice, pretending.

The track was joined by another that came up at a slant from the church. With a jolt of surprise, he saw, parked awkwardly under a mountain ash, a red car, a Fiesta – Nicole Whatsit's. She must have gone for a walk.

If he found her, he'd challenge her about the 20 pounds she owed. Maybe even get it from her, and go home triumphant – only most likely she wouldn't have the cash. He halted by the car, looked inside – nothing, only a road atlas on the front seat – then rode on, with a new sense of purpose. He scanned the tussocky slopes on both sides and ahead.

Funny, she didn't look like a walker. Usually they had Gore-Tex and map cases and big boots.

She looked like a town girl, with no walker's gear. Just her rucksack and – what sort of shoes? Trainers, he thought. Trainers were OK, but you needed boots for walking these rugged paths. In places you'd have to scramble. It could be slippy, if it rained. And it looked like raining now: the clouds were low, the air flecked with moisture. In his hurry to leave home, he hadn't thought of grabbing his coat.

There were disused mine shafts up here, not all of them fenced off. Serve her right, he caught himself thinking, if she blundered about with no map and ended up down one; but then he remembered her red-rimmed eyes and her furtive look. Like someone running away.

Well, he knew how that felt. He heard Dad's harsh voice, saw Mum's desperation; something twisted inside him like a stitch from running. He flapped the reins and kicked his heels. Obediently, the pony trotted forwards, stumbling once and almost pitching him over her shoulder. He grabbed the mane. Wouldn't want to fall off, up here, and let Tansy go. How could he tell Victoria – let alone her parents – that he'd lost the pony in the hills? But with his fingers twisted into the thickness of her mane he felt safer, and when the track evened out into a broad stretch of green, he pushed into a canter.

Cantering was easier than bumpy trotting; the rhythm was like being in a boat, or on a swing. He could get used to this riding business. Just him and a horse and the open hills – no need for lessons or Pony Club or all that prissy stuff. Tansy's hooves pounded the turf, her mane flew into his face. The wetness was in his hair, on his eyelashes; he laughed as sheep scattered in woolly panic.

At last the pony slowed, puffing. They'd come higher than Owen had realised, right into the cloud. It was so quiet; all he heard was the pony's breathing and his own, and the harsh *cra-aark* of a bird.

They walked into the mist.

He'd lost all sense of time. It had been quite early when he stomped out of the house, only just after breakfast; now he seemed to have ridden right out of the world below, just as he'd intended. He shivered, and turned up the collar of his rugby shirt. His legs clammed wetly to the saddle. Though there was no wind, it was colder up here than he'd imagined.

Dad sometimes talked about volunteering for Mountain Rescue, but was too busy with the shop to get round to it. Owen knew, from him, how easily people got into trouble in the hills. Especially unwary, unprepared people. "They park their car, see a nice track or a signpost, and off they go – no map or compass, no warm clothes, nothing to eat or drink," Dad had told him. "They've no idea how quick the cloud comes down, how soon things change. And with those mine shafts..."

Tansy would have more sense than to go near a mine shaft, wouldn't she? Ponies knew how to survive. But she was an Anglo-Arab, not a Welsh pony bred for the hills; and even sheep, who spent their whole lives up here, sometimes fell down the open chasms.

Perhaps he should trot again, to keep warm; but now the path was narrow and rock-strewn, dropping steeply on both sides. They'd reached a ridge, higher than he'd realised. He thought of turning back, but the pony was walking purposefully. Maybe she knew her way.

He'd get back down to safety, return the pony to her field, go home, and pretend he'd only been out for a walk. He needn't tell anyone.

Head down against the drizzle, he didn't even see what made the pony swerve violently. The next thing he knew, he was pitching over her shoulder, head down, legs whirling, hands grabbing; his shoulder slammed painfully against a rock. He rolled, gasped; regained his sense of which way was up; saw – in a fuzz of panic – Tansy trotting into the mist.

"Wait!" he yelled. He felt sick, shaken – even sicker at the thought of Victoria's pony lost up here in the cloud. He clutched his arm; he could still move it, so it wasn't damaged. Thank God for *that*.

"Tansy!" he shouted. He couldn't even see her. He felt blurry with shock.

"Who's that?" a voice called, somewhere above him. Like someone half-asleep, it sounded. He thought of roamers and apparitions in stories, lurers of travellers to their doom. He looked up: high on an outcrop, a dark figure loomed.

Owen's instinct was to turn down the slope

and run as fast as he could. But curiosity kept him still, staring. The figure came close to the edge, the height of a house roof above him, and crouched there looking down. It was just a small, ordinary person after all – a girl – not someone from a legendary time warp. He registered that it was the B&B girl, the girl he'd been looking for. Her lank hair swung as she peered down.

"What're you *doing*?" he asked, incredulous. Fancy sitting there in the rain! But first he must catch Tansy.

Some hope! She'd be halfway to Prestatyn by now. He floundered along the path that curved beneath the overhang. An awful warning floated into his mind: Victoria, saying, "You have to keep to the tracks. It's so rocky up there, a horse could break a leg."

Why hadn't he listened? The rain lashing into his face felt like a punishment. He wished he were safely at home, watching TV, doing *any*thing as long as he wasn't stranded up here, with a loose pony and a lunatic girl.

He saw the imprints of hooves in close-nibbled turf. Following, he caught his breath as he saw Tansy's white shape a few yards off. She'd stayed close, not taken advantage of her freedom after all. But she was edgy, throwing up her head as he approached.

"Come on, Tans. Good girl—" The reins dangled; she'd put one foot through them, and they caught round her foreleg when she raised her head. She seemed about to veer off, but stood snorting, letting him near enough to reach out a thankful hand for the reins. Stroking her neck, he felt dizzy with relief – alarmingly, close to tears. She could have galloped off anywhere, the whole of the Clwydian Hills to choose from! Lifting her foot, he freed the reins.

One problem solved; he felt heaviness dropping from him. Now the weird girl. He led the pony back to the overhang, half-expecting her to have vanished again. But there she was, watching from the ledge.

"Can't you get down?" Owen yelled.

"Too... cold..." It sounded as if her words were forced between clenched teeth.

Now what? Owen stood, undecided. He wanted to get back on Tansy and ride down, but he couldn't leave this gormless girl shivering here.

And she seemed incapable of helping herself.

"I'm coming up," he shouted.

First, he'd have to secure Tansy; couldn't risk her getting loose again. He fastened the reins round a boulder, rolling its weight to hold them. Now...

There was no way he could climb straight up; the jut of rock ledge made that impossible. But the girl had done it somehow. Skirting round behind, he saw a scrambly place that would do. He worked his way up, concentrating hard, testing each step.

A few minutes later he was standing on the flat table of rock, gazing in dismay at the girl. She was half-lying, looking down at Tansy, and shivering. She wore only jeans, trainers, and a thin sweatshirt that was soaked through.

It was dangerous to get cold and wet in the hills. Especially if you weren't moving about to keep warm. Especially if you were hungry – and this girl's Full English Breakfast was now progressing through his own digestive system. How long since *she'd* eaten?

People could die of exposure.

He shoved that notion into his brain.

She'll die unless you get her down. There's no one to help. Only you.

"Come on!" he ordered. "You've got to get moving." He grabbed her arm, and pulled her to her feet. She resisted, but stood weakly. Her eyes swivelled to face him. She looked awful: no colour in her face, her hair lank and dripping, her thin body shuddering.

"Walk!" he told her. "I'll show you the way."

It had been hard enough, scrambling up on his own; doubly so with this fragile girl to take care of. He started down, and called her after him.

Obstinately, she crouched on the edge, cuddling herself. "I can't!"

"Yes, you can! Turn round, and put your right foot here. Then your left one there. Hang on to that knobby bit."

He saw her wavering; knew he had to sound confident, even if he wasn't at all. Slowly, ditheringly, she did as he said.

"Good – now your right foot *here*. This ledge for your left. That's it." An hour seemed to have passed before she was down; and at once she collapsed in a huddle on the wet ground.

"That's it. I'm done in. I'm staying here." She gave him a brief, tearful look, and sat hugging her arms around her.

"Oh, don't be *stupid*!" In exasperation, Owen glanced round in all directions, as if Mountain Rescue teams might be pounding up the slopes. Of course, there was no one in sight.

"With exposure," Dad had told him, "what happens is you sit down to rest; and then you start to feel nice and warm. That's fatal. If you don't get up, you'll never get up again."

There was no alternative – he'd got to make her, somehow, stand up and walk. On an impulse, he fetched Tansy from her tethered place. Head down and miserable, she pawed the rock with her hoof, and shook water-droplets from her mane, impatient to move on.

He led her towards the shivering girl, who crouched small and shrunken against the rock. But she looked at the pony with a gleam of interest. "That yours?"

"No, I've only borrowed her. Her name's Tansy. Yours is Nicole, isn't it?"

"Nicole?" She looked puzzled. "Oh, right! You're from the B&B, aren't you?" She plucked at the sopping sleeve of her jumper. "Not really. I just said that—" She paused, and took a shuddering breath. "Like Nicole Kidman, you know? My real name's Heather."

She's demented, he thought. She must be!

"What brought you up here?"

She glared at him. "What's it to you?"

"Looks to me like you've completely lost it. First you walk out without paying—"

Heather wiped her eyes with a drooping sleeve. "I didn't! I did pay! Left the money by the lamp."

"Then you wander up here without even a *map*, no waterproofs or anything—" He'd done the same, but never mind. "People can die up here, without the proper gear. Don't you know? I mean, these aren't what you'd call real mountains, not like Snowdon and that, but still—"

"I know. I'm not stupid!"

"Well, then—" He looked at her, baffled. "D'you mean you wanted—?"

"No! Didn't mean to *die*. I just thought – like, I'd show them. You know?"

Yes. He knew.

"Show who?"

She swallowed hard. "My mum and dad. Just couldn't hack it any more. They think I'm a total failure. Hated school, walked out – can't stick at a job – split up with my boyfriend – can't get nothing right!" She made a gulping sound; her shoulders heaved. "So I got to the point, like, what *is* the point? Took my dad's car, and I haven't passed my test – can't even do that! And they won't come after me, will they, no one cares—"

"Look," Owen interrupted. "We've got to get moving."

Heather began to weep, wiping her nose on her sleeve. Owen looked helplessly at the sky. What now? What could he do if she collapsed in a sobbing heap? Tansy snorted, nudging her; the girl stood, hesitated, then flung both arms round the pony's neck, and cried and cried.

The pony waited quietly; Owen weighed up the possibilities. If he led Tansy, the girl would have to follow behind; there wasn't room for three of them to walk abreast. But he wasn't sure if he could trust her to keep coming.

Heather's sobs became hiccups; she stroked

the pony's mane. "She's nice. I always fancied riding. Never have, though. Only once on a donkey."

"You could ride now," Owen ventured.

She looked round at him, all snotty and bleary; she actually laughed. "You kidding? I'm clueless about horses."

And everything else, Owen thought; she could just about drive a car, but otherwise seemed as helpless as a baby.

"I'll show you. Look, you get on like this—"

It might be better, really, if she walked; that'd warm her up more quickly. But if she rode, they could at least get *moving*, and he wouldn't have to worry about her twisting an ankle, or giving him the slip.

Chilled, she was slow to pick things up. Owen felt like an expert as he showed her how to mount, then how to hold the reins. Tansy didn't seem to mind the change of rider; she set off willingly beside him.

But which way? The cloud was rolling down now, thick and swirling.

"Are we lost?" asked Heather, quite cheerfully.

Mum and Dad had the OS map at home. Owen wished he'd studied it more carefully. He had in mind that the sea was straight ahead; so the village would be somewhere down on their right. Or should they have gone the other way, further inland? Which way down, how steep were the slopes, where were the mine shafts?

"I'm starving," Heather announced.

"Yeah. I had your breakfast, didn't I."

"Didn't fancy it, then. I'd eat ten breakfasts now. Hang on." She sat back in the saddle, feeling in her jeans pocket, then handed him a piece of chewing gum and unwrapped one for herself. "Better'n nothing."

Owen chewed, relishing the sugary mintiness that faded all too quickly. But a little burst of sugar was better than nothing.

"I'm going to let the pony find the way down," he said. "Leave the reins loose and we'll go where she decides."

"You know what," Heather told him, "you're like one of those knights-in-armour, aren't you, King Arthur and them? Riding out of the mist on your white horse." She giggled. "Rescuing a damsel in distress."

Owen didn't feel at all knight-in-armourish: only drenched, chilled and with a rubbed heel that was beginning to blister. "Don't count on it. We're not down yet."

But Tansy was a better navigator than he was. Puzzled at first by the lack of guidance, she chose a steep downward track that made Heather sway and gasp, clutching the front of the saddle. Owen was unconvinced, wondering whether they shouldn't be further to the left; but while he was doubting, they reached a line of stunted trees beside a track, and heard the trickle of a stream. Then voices, shouting, and three blasts on a whistle.

They'd come to look for her. Heather's parents had reported her missing, and the red Fiesta had been seen and traced. The police called Mountain Rescue when they realised Heather had gone up into the hills; now her mum and dad were driving over from Wrexham. They'd been frantic, the policewoman said.

All this, Owen thought, while they'd thought themselves so lost and apart: all these phone calls and arrangements!

Everyone sat in the kitchen at home: Owen, and Heather, Mum and Dad, the two police, and a Mountain Rescue man. Tansy was in her stable; Owen had rubbed her down briefly and would see to her properly later on. He'd changed into dry clothes; Heather sat wrapped in a blanket, and Mum had brought out the fan heater. The kitchen was warm and steamy, and everyone was drinking hot chocolate.

Safe now, Heather was crying again, softly, almost soundlessly. Owen couldn't get her at all. Riding the pony, when they'd been together, the three of them, she'd changed her mood completely – been almost excited, like a kid at a funfair. Now she'd dissolved again into weeping.

Dad stood by the sink, concerned and puzzled, while the story unfolded; Mum fussed about, rubbing Owen's hands to check that he was warm enough, refilling his mug, offering biscuits to everyone.

"We've been so worried! Didn't know where you'd taken off to—"

"What I don't get," Dad said, "is how you knew where to look? And what made you think of taking the pony?"

Owen couldn't explain. Heather's crisis had made his own seem unimportant. And look at Mum and Dad now – no one would think they'd been snarling at each other just a few hours ago. Now they were a team, a family, offering warmth and comfort to strangers. They were *proud* of him, as if he'd done something brave or remarkable.

"Strikes me," said the policeman, "it's lucky for Heather that he did. She couldn't have survived long up there," he added in an undertone, as if everyone but Heather could hear. "People come to grief in milder weather than this."

Come to grief. Owen hadn't heard the phrase before, but he sat considering it. Heather had come here to *grieve* – and maybe she was doing it all in one dramatic burst. She'd shown that there was a more optimistic person inside. Maybe she'd got it out of her system.

Maybe he had, too.

Dad ruffled Owen's hair. "You're a bit of a hero, son! Riding to the rescue!"

Owen shook his head. There'd been nothing heroic about it. He couldn't even pretend that the stiffness in his shoulder was an honourable injury – he'd only fallen off a pony. And he'd have a lot of explaining to do: mainly to Victoria, about how he'd taken her pony without asking, and risked injuring or even losing her up in the hills.

But something had changed. For Heather, too: he hoped so. She'd said that no one cared, but her parents cared enough to report her missing, to be hurrying to fetch her home. Things could seem desperate, hopeless: but there were these strong cords that pulled you back and held you securely, even when you tried to cut them.

"Have another biscuit," said Mum. "You did put dry socks on, didn't you?"

"Mum – Dad," Owen said. "Could we go up in the hills sometimes, the way we used to – take lunch and a map, go for the whole day?"

Mum nodded. "It's been a while since we've done that."

"Should have thought you'd had enough of moors and mist," said the policewoman, laughing. "And it's not exactly picnic weather!"

But Dad smiled, and Owen knew that he

understood. The three of them, together, for a day out - that was what mattered. If the shop failed, if there were no B&B guests, if they were forever short of money – it wouldn't mean they had *nothing*. They would still be a family.

"Yes, of course we will," said Dad.

Finding My Roots

by Helen Williams

I live in Birmingham with my Jamaican dad and my English mum. Last summer, they sent me to spend my holidays with Aunt Merle and Uncle Duncan in Jamaica. It was my first visit there and my first time travelling alone.

As I scanned the faces outside Montego Bay Airport, I caught sight of a tall man, holding a piece of cardboard with my name on it in bold letters. The air hostess pushed me towards him.

"I'm Sashalee Bowen. Where's Aunt Merle and Uncle Duncan?" I asked.

"Your auntie's not well. I'm Sammy, their driver. They sent me to pick you up."

"Enjoy your holiday," said the hostess, squeezing my arm and vanishing into the crowd.

"And me is your great grandmother, Agatha Livingstone. Everybody call me Grandma

Aggie." The midget of a woman beside Sammy grabbed my hand. Her cheeks shone like polished ebony, but the rest of her skin was as wrinkled as a dry prune. "Come on. You keep us waiting too long." Her shrill voice sent shivers down my spine.

The porter pushed past with my luggage, following Sammy to the car. As I tagged along with my great grandmother, she said:

"Your aunt Merle had an asthma attack in Miami this morning, right before she shoulda go to the airport."

I got a sinking feeling in my stomach. I had been looking forward to spending some time with my aunt.

"No worries. Me will look after you."

Fifteen minutes later, we had passed the town with its well-lit streets, and veered to the left up a steep, dark road. More twists and turns took us further up the hill, then into a driveway. A blaze of sensor lights lit up a sprawling villa.

"See Merle's house here," said Grandma Aggie, climbing out of the car. Sammy opened the padlock on the grill gate and she ushered me inside.

I felt like I had stepped into a page out of a magazine. Beyond the spacious room was a patio bordering a pool, and lights twinkled in the distance. The sweet, heavy scent of jasmine drifted into the house.

"Velma! We reach," shouted Grandma Aggie. She cupped her hand over my ear and whispered, "One of me 30 grandchildren — your aunt Merle's helper."

"Miss Sashalee! You look even prettier than your picture!" A young woman stretched her work-worn hands towards me. "Your auntie said to call her as soon as you come." She dialled the number and passed me the phone.

"Hi, Aunt Merle."

"Hi, darling. I'm so sorry. Duncan won't let me travel until I'm fully recovered. And of course he couldn't leave without me. We'll be with you in a few days. Make yourself at home until then."

Velma showed me to my room and folded back the covers of the four-poster bed. I changed into my nightie and collapsed on to the soft mattress.

The next thing I knew, sunshine was streaming through the open louvre blades.

My watch said 12 o'clock, which meant it was six in the morning, Jamaica time.

I went out on to the patio. Beside the pool were tall palm trees and, way beyond the lawn, the sea glinted in the morning light. To the left was luxuriant vegetation; to the right, in the distance, Montego Bay sprawled over grey-green hills. A hummingbird was feeding on red flowers near the pool.

"You going spend all day staring?" Grandma Aggie gripped my shoulder with her bony fingers.

"No, Grandma Aggie, I'm going to swim." I dashed back to my room, changed into a bikini and grabbed a towel.

"Where you going in your underwear?" Grandma Aggie squealed. Had she never seen a bikini before?

"Right here." I dipped a toe in the pool. The water felt so warm, I jumped in and swam a few laps. A whole pool to myself! This was the life.

"Why don't you come for a swim, Grandma Aggie?"

"That's a good joke!" she cackled. "Come have your breakfast. We soon leave."

I sat beside her at a table on the patio. "Where are we going?" I asked, between mouthfuls of cornflakes.

"Since Merle not here, you can come spend time with me."

"Grandma will frighten you with duppy story," warned Velma.

"Me tell duppy story and do other things, so children learn how to behave." Grandma Aggie winked at me.

"What's a duppy?" I asked.

"A ghost-somebody's spirit. There's plenty of them way up in the country where she live," said Velma. "You not going like it there. She don't have no light or water."

"Don't listen to Velma. Me know you been camping. You enjoy it?" I nodded. "Then you going like staying with me." She had a mischievous look in her twinkling eyes. "Latoya will keep you company."

"Who's Latoya?"

"Another great granddaughter."

"Grandma's right hand," said Velma.

"Cho. Me can manage on me own."

"So why you work her so hard?"

"To keep her out of mischief," said Grandma Aggie.

"How old is she?" I asked.

"Thirteen, same age as you."

"I'm 11."

"Me is 88." She pushed her face towards me. "If you don't come stay with me now, you might not see me house till me funeral."

"Stop that foolishness," said Velma.

In spite of Velma's forebodings, I was curious to see where my great grandmother lived and to hear more about the duppies. I wanted to look for my roots in Jamaica, too. Grandma Aggie's might be the best place. I certainly wouldn't find them in Aunt Merle's swimming pool.

"I'll come," I said. I looked at Velma. She was shaking her head.

Grandma Aggie gave her a triumphant smile.

The road to Grandma Aggie's house snaked up into the mountains. At first there were houses and shops, then these gave way to trees and patches of cultivated ground clinging to the steep slopes at the sides of the road. Sammy had to drive slowly because of the potholes.

As we neared the district where Grandma Aggie lived, the road was more hole than surface. Sammy brought the car to a halt beside a small gate. Carrying our bags, he went ahead of us up a short path leading to a wooden house.

"Uncle Sammy!" A girl rushed on to the porch and grabbed his hand. He hugged her.

"Sashalee, what time for you tomorrow?" Sammy said.

"She not leaving tomorrow," snapped Grandma Aggie.

Sammy snorted. "When you've had enough of this woman, call me to come for you. Plenty people round here have cell phones." He handed me a slip of paper with his number, and turned to leave. In two strides, he was back at the car.

"Sashalee, meet Latoya," said Grandma Aggie.

"Hi, Sashalee. Welcome home." Latoya grinned. She was taller than me, but slimmer. Her hair, like mine, was plaited in cane rows. She wore a pair of shorts and a sleeveless blouse tied in a knot at her waist. Her feet were bare.

Five minutes later, Grandma Aggie had changed into a T-shirt and faded, checked skirt.

"Get you'selves ready," she commanded. "We going to the bush." She wrapped her frizzy, grey hair in a bandana, and put on a pair of rubber boots. She picked up a machete and baskets and, without waiting for us, marched up the path leading from the backyard.

As I followed with Latoya, she showed me banana plants; rough-skinned, round, green breadfruit; and cocoa trees with shiny, brown pods. My eyes wide, I drank in images of plants I had seen only in pictures. As the path became steeper, I was puffing and panting, trying to keep up. Then we came out into a clearing at the top of the hill.

"You like me view?" Grandma Aggie was waiting for us.

I gasped. In front of me, valleys and hills dotted with houses and covered in lush green vegetation, cultivated here and forested there, stretched way into the distance. In another direction were hump-shaped, tree-clad mountains. Somewhere beyond, the huge expanse of sky overhead met the ocean.

"Time for work." Grandma Aggie broke into my thoughts. She showed me yam vines with heart-shaped leaves twisting around sticks put there for that purpose.

My job was to pull out the weeds growing between them. Meanwhile, Latoya used a machete to build up the rich soil round the base of the yam stems, in much the same way as Dad earthed up potatoes.

Soon, tired and feeling terribly hot from working in the mid-morning sun, I stopped to drink water.

"Latoya, how long have you lived with Grandma Aggie?" I asked.

"My whole life. Mama was living with her when I was born."

"Where's your mum now?"

"She went to England three years ago. She wants me to join her next year." She glanced at Grandma Aggie, reaping yams some distance from us.

"Look as though you're working," warned Latoya. "That great grandmother of ours has been giving me a hard time since Mama told her I'll be leaving. She won't admit it, but she's afraid of getting sick with nobody to look after her."

My hands were soon sore and my muscles weak from this new exertion. Perhaps I would ask Sammy to come for me tomorrow, after all.

When the sun was overhead, we returned to the house. To my amazement, Latoya and Grandma Aggie balanced the baskets of yams on their heads. We stopped on the way to gather wood for the fire; to pick hot peppers and a breadfruit. Back at Grandma Aggie's, we went into the kitchen, which was in a small, wooden building detached from the house.

Latoya spread laundry soap on the outside of a large pot, half-filled it with water, and set it above the fire. Grandma Aggie put a piece of salted pork into the pot, then she sat on a bench at the counter, peeling yam and breadfruit. Latoya cut some green bananas off a bunch leaning in the corner. She peeled them and put them into the pot, too. She spoke to Grandma Aggie in rapid-fire patois, but to me she spoke slowly in perfect English.

At about two o'clock, the food was ready.

"Eat plenty," she said, serving me. "This is dinner, the main meal of the day." She poured

me a drink made from limes and brown sugar —
they called it lemonade.

Usually, I don't like trying new food, but I was ravenous. And, to my surprise, I enjoyed the meal. The texture of the breadfruit was more like potato than bread. The pork tasted like ham, with a spicy flavour.

"Some pepper?" Latoya put a fingernail-sized piece on my plate.

"Careful," said Grandma Aggie.

I tasted it, gingerly. It was like fire! Latoya laughed as I cooled my mouth with lemonade.

After dinner, Grandma Aggie went to lie down.

"Does Grandma Aggie frighten you with duppy stories?" I asked Latoya.

"She did when I was little."

"I'd like to hear one."

"You sure? Ask her this evening, after dark."

As we spoke, I washed the plates and cups while Latoya scoured the pot with some rough grass and ashes. The soot from the fire came off easily because of the soap she'd put on it.

"I bet you don't work as hard as me," said Latoya, "with these chores to do every day."

"No, I only help Mum on weekends," I said, lamely.

"What's England like?" she asked.

"It's OK in summer, but you won't like the winter — it's wet and cold."

"What do you do with yourself?"

"Go shopping; go to the cinema; chat with friends online."

"That must be fun. Do you like to read?"

I nodded. Later, we exchanged storybooks and sat outside, reading.

In the evening, after a supper of sweet cornmeal porridge flavoured with nutmeg, we sat on the porch, watching the golden glow in the sky turn purple, then blue-black.

"Grandma Aggie, tell me about my dad's family," I said.

"Me have eight children — four boys and four girls." She took a deep breath. "There was Ronald — Latoya's grandpa, and Weston, and Astley, and Ruby, me eldest daughter—"

"She's my granny," I interrupted.

"Yes, she go a England when her daughter Merle was four and Trevor, your papa, was two.

Left me to care for them. Me was still raising me own children."

"Like Dad's aunt Joyce? He told me she helped you look after him."

"Yes, she's me youngest child. You'll meet her tomorrow. Where we reach? Ah, yes, I was raising your papa. When he turn 15, he and Merle go a England to their mama. Merle did nursing. That's how she meet her doctor-husband."

A rap at the gate drew our attention to three visitors, who joined us on the porch.

"Sashalee?" I nodded. "Me is Weston, this old lady's favourite boy. And these are me sons, George and Frankie."

I shook their calloused hands. They were drinking beer and put a bottle on the table for Grandma Aggie. She drank thirstily, then wiped her lips with the back of her hand.

Latoya hung an oil lamp on a hook above the table, and Frankie tipped out a box of dominoes.

"George, you playing with me?" Grandma Aggie rubbed her hands together and winked at him.

While the domino game took place, I asked Latoya if Ronald, her grandpa, lived nearby.

"He died before I was born. A tractor fell on top of him and killed him."

"How horrible!" I shuddered.

"That's why my granny went back to Kingston, the capital, with her children. But my mama stayed here, with Grandma Aggie, to keep her company."

The players made so much noise, slapping their dominoes on the table, we could hardly hear ourselves think. We turned our attention to the game. Grandma Aggie and George won, amid more banging of dominoes and shouting.

"Another game?" she asked.

"We're working men. We have to get to market early tomorrow. You have anything for us to take?"

Latoya went for the box of yam, peppers and bananas.

After they left, Latoya said, "Grandma Aggie, Sashalee wants to hear a duppy story."

"A duppy story, eh?" With a gleam in her eye, Grandma Aggie began. "When me was your age,

Mama send me with breadfruit for me uncle. She tell me, 'Don't let night catch you on the road'. But me stop and play with me cousins and before me know it, darkness come down. Me walk fast, then me hear a chain clanking. Lord have mercy! A rollin' calf! Worst kind of duppy! Me look back and see a pair of blazing, red eyes. Me never run so fast in me whole life."

"How frightening!" I shivered.

The next morning, our first task was to go to the standpipe for water. While we waited our turn, people stared at me. In a few moments, a crowd had surrounded me.

"She white, eh?" somebody whispered. In Birmingham, I was called a half-caste and told to go back to where I came from. Now I felt like an animal in a zoo — blank faces staring at me, saying nothing.

"This is Sashalee, Trevor's daughter from England," announced Latoya.

The faces creased into smiles and everybody started talking at once.

A middle-aged woman took my hand, saying, "From me see you, me know who you is. Me is your papa's aunt Joyce. How him doing? Me no see him this long time."

"He's fine, Aunt Joyce." Although she was my great-aunt, I dropped the word "great", as was the custom. "Dad told me to tell you 'hello'."

Having filled the plastic buckets and bottles with water, Latoya heaved them on to a wooden trolley, and we trundled it back to our house.

From that time, anywhere I went in the district, people stopped me to tell me how they were related to me, and that I must remember them to my papa.

A few days later, Aunt Joyce let me use her cell phone to call Aunt Merle.

"Stay as long as you're happy," said Aunt Merle. "Don't let Grandma force you to do anything you don't want."

"I'm having fun with Latoya," I told her. "I love the goats and the chickens; and eating the food we grow; and cooking over a fire."

"Are you sure? Well, call me when you want Sammy to come."

Although my hands were blistered and my muscles were aching, and I did feel a little bit homesick, Latoya turned every hardship into a joke. I guess that's how she coped, especially in term time when she had to go to school in Montego Bay every day.

Saturday was cleaning day and Sunday was church, so we didn't go to the bush. We had Sunday lunch — chicken and rice'n'peas — at Aunt Joyce's house, with her husband, a daughter, three grandchildren and two nephews. Aunt Joyce had a concrete-block house with electricity, and a water tank. After lunch, somebody turned on the television.

"Latoya has work to do," said Grandma Aggie, getting to her feet. "Me don't want night to catch her on the road."

Latoya and I exchanged glances.

That evening, as we went to take the goats in from their grazing, I asked Latoya, "Did night ever catch you on the road?"

"Many times," she said.

"Did you ever see a duppy?"

Latoya's eyes crinkled at the corners and she shook her head.

"I want to see one before I go home."

"You must be crazy."

"Not crazy, just curious."

Latoya covered her mouth, stifling a laugh. "It's full moon, so there'll be no rollin' calf, but I do have an idea. I have to check with some cousins first. And I warn you, if Grandma Aggie finds out, we'll feel her tamarind switch."

"Grandma Aggie beats you?"

"Oh, yes. Her favourite saying is 'Spare the rod and spoil the child'. She hasn't raised any spoilt children, I can tell you."

On Tuesday evening, after we'd gone to bed, Latoya nudged me.

"You still want to see a duppy?"

"Yes."

Leaving Grandma Aggie snoring, we pulled on our clothes and slipped out of the house.

The moon was well above the horizon, the trees casting eerie shadows. At the crossroads, singing came from the church; and the sound of merriment and the clack of dominoes came from the bar.

"Is it safe?" I asked, as we turned left along a lonely road.

"You scared? There's safety in numbers." She glanced behind her. About 20 children were following us. Our cousins. A mile further on, we turned up the driveway to an old great-house.

"Stop here," said Latoya. "Sashalee, lie down."

"What?"

"Lie down. You want to see a duppy, don't you?"

I lay down and stared at the sky. My heart was beating a mile a minute. The children ran back and forth. I opened my eyes wider, but I didn't see anything.

"Lift up your hands," said Latoya. She hauled me up and I took two steps forwards. "Look behind you." On the ground was the shape of my body outlined in the pebbles the children had put down. "There's your duppy!" The children doubled up, suppressing their laughter.

"That's it?" What a rotten trick she had played on me!

"We're not done." She beckoned the children and we all hid behind a hedge. I took a quick look at my duppy. The moonlight bouncing off the stones did give it a ghostly appearance.

No one spoke. After some minutes, we heard voices and the click of shoes on the driveway. Two women appeared. As they caught sight of my duppy, they let out ear-piercing screams, threw their hands in the air, and ran off in the direction from which they had come. The children choked on their snorts until they burst out as deep belly laughs, filling the night air.

"Hush!" said Latoya. "Mind somebody hear."

The children huddled together behind the hedge, listening.

"What's that sound?" I whispered. Before anybody could answer, the children leapt to their feet. A chain was rattling nearby.

"Rollin' calf," they yelled and dashed off down the road, like a stream of bubbles. I wrapped my arms around Latoya, holding her down.

"You said rollin' calf is afraid of moonlight."

"Y-y-es," she stuttered.

"I want to see this."

"You're m-m-ad."

We were both shaking and I felt as though my heart was going to thump out of my chest. The rattling got louder. We didn't dare look. When it was right beside us, I peeked over the hedge. A familiar figure, dragging a chain along the ground, kicked my "duppy" as she passed.

"Latoya, look! It's Grandma Aggie," I hissed.

Latoya's eyes nearly popped out of her head. We sank to the ground behind the hedge, too surprised to laugh.

"We're in big trouble. Some kid must have told on us." Latoya grabbed hold of my arm. Even though we kept our distance behind Grandma Aggie as we followed her, there was no escape.

She had her tamarind switch ready for us as we entered the house.

"You think you is big woman, eh?" Grandma Aggie shouted, grabbing Latoya's arm and bringing the switch down, stinging her legs. Latoya drew in her breath sharply, bracing for the next strike.

I trembled at the prospect of my fate. My parents had never beaten me for misbehaving and I felt so ashamed, having brought this punishment on the two of us.

"I'm sorry, Grandma Aggie," said Latoya.

"Me too," I choked on my words.

"Sorry, eh?" She lowered the tamarind switch. "Me sorry Sashalee's not my child to beat, and me can't give Latoya a proper beating with her here."

We both breathed sighs of relief.

Latoya and I woke the next morning to find Grandma Aggie ready to go to the bush. We rushed to finish our chores and were preparing to go with her, when a car horn sounded. Aunt Merle marched up to the house.

"Grandma phoned me earlier to tell me you're giving her trouble. Both of you, pack up your things and get in the car, while I talk to her."

In a moment, we were sitting behind Sammy, waiting nervously. At last, Aunt Merle came out, smiling.

"I've had a long talk with Grandma and she's forgiven you." I gasped. "Sashalee, you need to understand that Grandma is an old-time Jamaican. She doesn't tolerate being disrespected." I hung my head. "But, in spite of everything, I want you to enjoy the rest of your holiday." Sammy started the car. "And since you two have become inseparable, Grandma is allowing Latoya to come with us on a tour of Jamaica." We shrieked and hugged each other, and fell off the seat when the car lurched round the next corner.

"What about Grandma Aggie?" asked Latoya.

"Joyce will find a young man to help on her farm, and a sensible woman to stay with her."

In the weeks that followed, we stayed in real hotels, and swam in the warm Caribbean; we climbed waterfalls; we watched daredevils jumping off cliffs into the sea. Sailing up the Black River, we saw crocodiles; rafting on the Martha Brae River, we saw an old sugar mill. Everybody we met was friendly and kind to us. Latoya was in seventh heaven, experiencing for the first time the Jamaica she had only read about. Her joy was infectious. Like hummingbirds feeding, she and I darted from one thrilling discovery to the next.

One day, on our travels, Aunt Merle made a suggestion. "Latoya, my dear, how would you like to board with us during the week? It would be easier for you to go to school from our house. You could go to Grandma's on weekends."

Latoya opened her eyes wide in disbelief.

"That's a wonderful idea," I said. "And by the time you leave for England, Grandma will be used to living without you."

Our holiday over, we took Latoya home.

Grandma Aggie hugged us. "Sashalee, me child, come back soon," she said.

While Aunt Merle talked to her, Latoya and I took our last chance to be together, just the two of us. At the yam ground, I could hardly believe how much the vines had grown in the three weeks we'd been away. As I looked at the view, I saw in my mind's eye, beyond the mountains, all the places we'd visited on our trip.

Latoya took hold of my hand. I squeezed hers.

"Will you come back?" she asked.

"We *both* will. We have to." And it was true. I had found my roots here, and stems and branches, too — a whole new family stretching across the miles and back through the ages. I had come home.

Christmas with Auntie Annie Ping Pong

by Tim Wynne-Jones

Auntie Annie Ping Pong had lost her marbles.

"It could be worse," said Jack's mother. "Some people as elderly as Annie are handicapped, bedridden, depressed... At least she's happy."

Jack watched Auntie Annie Ping Pong handing a cup of tea to a vase of flowers.

"There's no one there," he said, politely.

She looked up, a smile breaking out on her face. "Oh, there you are, Jack," she said. "I was just telling Candace here what a fine lad you were."

Jack turned away and secretly rolled his eyes. Candace was Annie's sister. She lived in England. Then he watched Annie pour another cup of tea. This one was for the lamp.

"Now, drink up, Maurice," said Annie, poking

the lamp. "It's got two sugars, just the way you like it."

"Auntie Annie," said Jack. "Your brother Maurice has been dead for 26 years."

Annie scowled good-naturedly. "Well, that's no reason for him to be rude," she said.

Auntie Annie Ping Pong wasn't really Jack's aunt; she was a great-aunt. But his family were the only relatives she had nearby. So they were the ones who arranged for help and took her to her doctors' appointments, kept up her many prescriptions and looked in on her. Jack came over to her flat every day after school, and stayed there until his mother finished work.

It used to be fun. Annie used to feed him homemade Welsh cake and shortbread and Coke, which he wasn't allowed at home. Then they would play cards or watch soaps and boo the bad guys.

But not any more. No more baking; his father had taken the fuses out of Annie's stove so she couldn't hurt herself. And no more cards; Annie thought all the cards were people. One day she had a long conversation with the three of clubs.

Auntie Annie Ping Pong wasn't her real name, but she had always been that to Jack. And now, when he thought about it, it seemed perfect. Talking to Annie was like a ping-pong match. They could keep the ball in the air only for so long, before *Plop*! – it would roll off the table, *Zing*! – it would bounce off the ceiling, *Flub*! – it got snagged in the net.

"Don't let it get you down," said Jack's father. "At least these hallucinations of hers are friendly."

They were friendly, all right. He watched Annie place a little lavender-coloured pillow behind a fruit bowl. "Are you comfy, dear?" she asked. She patted a shiny apple on the head.

"You're talking to an apple," said Jack, trying to sound patient.

Annie smiled at him and then smiled at the apple, too, as though they were all having a good time together.

Her neighbours in the apartment block were great. She left the door of her flat unlocked and they popped in for visits.

"She came around to our place today," said Mr Morcombe to Jack one afternoon. "Seems her 'visitors' were asleep on her bed and she couldn't take a nap. So I sent them packing."

"Thanks," said Jack. He smiled respectfully.

"No problemo," said Mr Morcombe. "We all love our Annie."

Which is when Jack thought a horrible thing: *If you all love her so much, why don't* you *look after her*? Of course, he didn't say it. These days he was full of things he didn't dare say.

He started sneaking around to Annie's back door to avoid neighbourly confrontations. Auntie Annie lived on the ground floor. There was a deck with steps down to the garden. She seldom went out any more, not even to church. And she never went out alone.

"I'm a little uncertain on my pins," she said, leaning heavily on her walker.

Jack remembered when he had to run to keep up with her. It made him sad.

Some days were worse than others. Once he arrived after school to find her at the counter in the kitchen. "You're here," she said, with a worried look on her face. "My muscles are on holiday today, Jack. Perhaps you can cut this sandwich."

"Sure thing," said Jack, and helped her to a seat at the table.

But he couldn't cut the sandwich. Because, apart from the cheese, lettuce, mayonnaise and tomato, the sandwich also contained the TV remote. It was a TV-remote sandwich with the works!

Jack didn't say anything. He took out the remote and handed Auntie Annie the sandwich cut up into quarters.

She took a bite and looked thoughtful. "Hmmm, it seems to be missing something."

"Don't laugh," said Jack to his parents at dinner that night. "Can't they give her some drugs or something?"

"She's already on a dozen drugs," said his father. "They're part of the problem. Especially the Prednisone for her Temporal Arteritis. But without it, she might have a stroke."

Jack pushed the potatoes around his plate, gloomily. He had spent half an hour trying to get the gunk out of the TV remote. When Annie had asked him what he was doing, he said, "I'm digging Cheddar cheese out of your TV remote, Auntie Annie."

"Oh," she said, chuckling merrily. "That sounds fun."

"Shouldn't she be in a home, or something?" Jack said, irritably. "Then she would have real people to talk to, instead of talking to the furniture. Or making sandwiches out of it."

His mother patted his hand. "I know it's weird, but try to see the bright side of things. She's got a care worker coming in twice a day, Meals on Wheels bringing her hot lunches, and good neighbours. As long as her delusions are harmless, she's just as well off where she is."

But Jack wasn't so sure her delusions were harmless. Some days she was pretty jumpy.

"It's these guests," she said to him, one cold November afternoon. "I can't get them to leave. What am I going to feed them?"

Jack had an idea. "Your guests are imaginary," he said softly. "They can make their own imaginary food."

She looked pleased, but then she frowned. "Well, just as long as they don't make any smelly stuff like fish."

December rolled around. It snowed, and every fat flake whispered Christmas.

When Jack arrived at the flat one day, he found Auntie Annie out on her porch with just a sweater over her shoulders, staring at the garden and the river beyond. Quickly, he hustled her inside and wrapped a blanket around her. She kept staring out of the window, preoccupied.

"What's up?" he asked.

Aunt Annie looked confused. "Is this a test?" she asked. "I've had so many tests lately."

"No," said Jack, "it's not a test."

But Auntie Annie wasn't listening, she was thinking. Then she smiled. "Can you hear?" she said. "Gloria Boemkamp is up. Those are her footsteps." She beamed with pride. She made Jack listen and, sure enough, Mrs Boemkamp was walking around upstairs.

Jack shook his head, tried not to scream with frustration and took himself off to watch TV in Auntie Annie's bedroom. He couldn't cope. But a few minutes later, she was at the bedroom door, wringing her hands.

"What is it?" Jack asked, a little frightened by the look on her face.

"They're still there," she said. "I think we had better invite them in."

"Who?" said Jack.

"The two fellows at the bottom of the garden by the river. They've been there all day. They must be very cold."

Jack went to look.

Auntie Annie followed him. "Oh," she said. "There's three of them now."

The riverbank was empty but for the tall grass and reeds dusted with new snow. Annie opened the sliding door, letting in a gust of icy wind. Jack closed the door, quickly. But not quickly enough. Annie was already addressing her latest guests.

"Did you come by boat?" she asked.

The three imaginary strangers were still there the next day. None of them had drunk their tea, but Annie was in high spirits. "They don't like plain old everyday tea," said Auntie Annie to Jack when he arrived that afternoon. "So I brewed a pot of Darjeeling."

She didn't seem anxious, any more, but Jack was. "Do you think it's wise to let strangers in?" he asked, trying to be diplomatic.

Annie looked towards the china cabinet. Apparently that was where the three men congregated. She had offered them a seat, she told Jack, but they had things to talk about in private.

"Well, I wouldn't normally, of course," said Annie. "But you see they have to wait somewhere. And I feel I almost know them," she added.

"Wait for what?" said Jack. It sounded ominous to him.

But Annie only looked delighted. "For Christmas, Jack. What else?"

"Why didn't I think of that?" said Jack.

Then Annie excused herself. "Which reminds me," she said, as she motored off in her walker. "I'd better get started on my knitting."

She returned with her knitting bag. Jack hadn't seen her knit in ages. Her arthritis was usually too bad. Now she seemed raring to go.

"What do you think?" she said, taking her favourite seat by the window. "Blue or pink?" She held up two thick balls of pastel-coloured yarn.

Jack was at a loss. "What do *they* think?" he said gesturing towards the china cabinet.

Annie laughed. "Oh, them." she said,

dismissing the strangers with a wave of her hand. Then she dug out a ball of creamy-white wool. "I'll go with white," she said. "Better safe than sorry."

"Annie?" said Jack. "What would you say if I told you I don't see anyone in the corner? No one at all."

Annie looked at him with kindly eyes. "I'd say you should see someone about your vision."

"How about I walk home after school from now on?" said Jack to his mother in the car that night. This was a joke. They lived in the country, 12 miles from Annie's flat. "I just can't keep it up!" he cried.

"Christmas is coming," said Jack's mother, trying to make him feel better. "Auntie Bridget and her family will be here and you'll get a well-deserved break."

"Annie's already got more visitors than she can handle," said Jack. He stamped his foot. "Why can't I convince her they're not real?"

They drove in silence for a moment, the snow swirling into phantom forms in the darkness before them. And then Jack's mother said, "Well, they are real to her, Jack. It's hard to argue with someone about something they think they can see." Jack didn't respond. Then his mother said, "She's in such a good mood. And knitting, too. Play along if you can. OK?"

Jack turned to the back seat piled high with groceries. "You hear that, guys?" he said. "We've got to play along."

His mother laughed. "That's the spirit," she said.

And he did play along.

Auntie Annie Ping Pong was deep in conversation with the three strangers when Jack arrived the next day. "They're magicians," she said.

Jack waved at the china cabinet. "Hi, guys," he said. "Can you do some disappearing tricks?"

"I'm sure they can," said Annie, knitting away, her gnarled fingers going a mile a minute. "They were doing card tricks earlier. And one of them, Gaspar, made a gold coin come out of my ear."

"Caspar," said Jack. "The friendly ghost?"

Annie laughed. "Don't be silly, dear, I said 'Gaspar'. And the tall one is Balthazar and the other's got such a thick accent I can't get his name, so I call him Norman. Now, why don't you go and see how the others are doing?"

The others?

The TV was blaring in Annie's bedroom. Wrestling was on. Jack watched for a moment as Goldilocks Gabor pinned Herod the Horrible to the floor. Then Jack noticed that there were cups of tea strewn all over the bedroom. And plates of bsicuits. There was even a plate on the floor. He picked up one of the biscuits. It was still warm. It was one of Annie's shortbreads, a little too brown on top, but still very good.

In the kitchen, he checked the oven; it wasn't hot. But the toaster oven was.

"Good shortbread," said Jack, rejoining Annie in the living room.

She smiled appreciatively, the skin around her eyes crinkling.

"You're kind to say so," she said. "They're a little dry. But you see, I had to do something, with all these new folks arriving. And their dogs, too."

"Ah, dogs. That explains the biscuits on the floor."

She nodded. Then she stopped knitting for a

minute and looked puzzled. "What are those things going 'Baaaaa'?" she asked.

"Sheep," said Jack.

"They might be sheep," said Annie.

"Sheep," said Jack, again. Hmmm, he thought. This was getting interesting. He sat at Annie's feet watching her knit and said, "That looks like a blanket. Is somebody having a baby?"

"That's what they say," said Annie, gesturing with her busy needles towards the strangers.

"The magicians?" he asked.

"That's right," said Annie.

"Are they sort of like wise men?" said Jack.

"Oh, they certainly seem so," said Annie. Then she leaned forwards and whispered to Jack. "Actually, they can be a bit snooty at times." Jack sniggered and Annie told him to keep quiet. "They've probably got a lot on their mind," she added.

"I bet," said Jack.

Annie's eyes twinkled. She had once been a first-class twinkler. Jack had almost forgotten. Lately, her eyes looked foggy, on account of all her medication. But they looked twinkly now, and it was as welcome to Jack as the smell of baking. Suddenly he felt good. He had a pretty good idea of what was going on, and he was full of things he *could* say.

"The ones in the bedroom watching wrestling. Do you think maybe they're shepherds?"

Annie paused. "Yes," she said. "Except I think one of them said he was an electrician. Oh, and I just remembered," she added excitedly. "Some of them are angels, Jack. You just ask."

Jack nodded. "It makes sense," he said. "I mean, with the wings and everything." And then he had a great idea. "So how about we make them something special?"

Jack put the fuses back into the oven and set it at the right temperature for Angel Food Cake. It was one of Annie's specialities. She didn't need a recipe. She hummed a little song while she worked and she got around fine on her pins, Jack noticed. He separated the eggs. It wasn't easy.

When Jack's mother came, they had to wait for the cake to finish baking. Jack introduced his mother to the wise men and the gang in the bedroom who were watching *The Simpsons* now, the Christmas special.

Finally, inevitably – although it always seems to take for ever – Christmas Eve rolled into town. Jack's aunt Bridget arrived from Liverpool. A limp and wretched little tree was found in town and made presentable with decorations. Presents appeared from nowhere to go under it.

Annie looked flushed and a little perplexed. "It's going to be very crowded," she whispered to Jack. He knew what she meant.

Then Bridget said, wouldn't it be nice if they all went to Midnight Mass together.

Annie had to sit down. She looked bewildered. "Oh, but I can't," she said.

"Please come," said Bridget. "You always love that service."

Annie started wringing her hands. She appealed to Jack with her eyes.

"It's OK," he said. Then he explained to Bridget and her husband Bob, and his cousins Ray and Sylvia, why Annie had to stay behind.

His cousins looked around them with alarm. "You get used to it," said Jack, understandingly.

At Annie's suggestion, he introduced everyone to the wise men, the shepherd, the sheep, the angels and the electrician. Then everybody went to church. Everybody except Auntie Annie Ping Pong and Jack. They stayed behind and waited, Annie at the window, Jack pacing.

Then, a little after 11, with a gasp of delight, Annie flung open the sliding door. "You two must be exhausted!" she said, as she welcomed the invisible travellers inside.

Jack watched with fascination as Annie led her latest imaginary guests to the bedroom, making small talk the whole way, about the weather and the trip and taxes and how Mary was holding up. Jack found himself suddenly *wishing* he could see what she could see.

He sat there alone by the Christmas tree. After a bit, he got up and went to the door. It was a cold night. He thought maybe he'd better let the donkey in or give it some hay, or something.

He laughed to himself. Here he was playing the game. It was easier when you knew the story. Christmas had given him a script.

But what would happen after Christmas? There was a lot of life left in Annie.

Oh well, he thought. Whatever. But he knew he would keep finding the ball and putting it back in play: ping pong, ping pong, ping pong.

There was no donkey on the deck, of course. But there was a winter moon and a fresh supply of air, gift wrapped with stars. Revived and shivering, Jack stepped back into the warmth of Annie's apartment.

He went to check up on her. She was sitting in a corner of her bedroom lit by a dim light, her hands folded together under her chin, staring lovingly at the blanket she had made, which lay in the middle of her bed.

She looked up at Jack. "Isn't the baby exquisite?" she whispered.

Jack looked at the bed. There was no one there that he could see. But when he looked at Auntie Annie, there was a miracle all right.

It was in her eyes.

116

After the Storm
by Kim Kitson

Tommy glanced at the sky. He could smell the rain. Not hail though, at least, by the look of the clouds. He lifted the hammer.

Just a few more nails to finish the decking. A last coat of paint tomorrow.

He squinted down the line of the boat.

Not as good as Dad would do, but not bad.

He frowned.

Pity about the colour. Still, beggars can't be choosers, as Dad always said. Anyway, gold is for champions. What was the other thing? Show me the cheapest one, and I'll learn to love it.

Everyone laughed when Tommy's dad said that. Tommy didn't think it was funny; it just sounded like the right thing to do. But he always smiled so people would know he was keeping up with everything. He sighed.

You could get used to anything, given time.

The boat bobbed in the rising wind and Tommy began to slap nails into the wood. He looked at the clouds on the horizon.

Stay away rain. I have to finish the top coat tomorrow.

He glanced up at the cottage at the edge of the bush. Someone had turned on the outside light, even though it wasn't really dark.

Dad wouldn't like that. Waste of electricity.

A car gunned into the street. Doors slammed. The sounds of his family drifted down the headland. Tommy packed away the hammer and nails and slipped off the side of the boat into the water. He checked the mooring rope then, holding the tool box above his head, he waded to the beach.

Tommy could see a figure staring down at him from the sand dunes. Mad: his cousin. Her real name was Magdelene, but she hated it, even though she once told him it meant "mighty battle maiden". She was the youngest of six, and three years older than Tommy, though you'd never know it, the way she screamed and shouted at the world. She didn't seem to notice there were never any gaps for him when she talked. She told him yesterday he was going to live with her family after the funeral.

I don't want to live with all of them. No way. Grandpa might not know much about three veg, homework every night and ironing, but he knows everything about Dad and computers and hot chocolate when you can't sleep.

Tommy dropped the tool box on the sand. He yelled he didn't want any help and could she just give him five minutes' peace, but Mad was already skimming over the beach, laughing and kicking up sand. For once, Tommy didn't chase her. He picked up his things and trudged up the beach in his cousin's scattered footsteps, past the flame trees with their dripping red blooms and up to the cottage, which was full of people.

Grandpa was waiting for Tommy as he scuffed the sand off his feet at the back door. "All right, lad?"

"I've still got a bit to do."

"There's time, Tommy, loads of time."

"I remember everything Dad told me. I just wanted to finish..." Tommy chewed his lip.

Grandpa bent down to look into his eyes. "I know, Tommy lad, but remember, I'm a man of leisure, a free spirit. Not tied to all that studying any more. I'll be here to help."

Tommy nodded, but he knew it wasn't true. Grandpa was always out. When Grandma died four years ago, he had sat in his armchair watching the sea for weeks. Then, one morning, he walked down the bush track to town and bought a computer. Grandpa had surfed the Net through the night for months. He began signing up for courses that ended when pale-yellow certificates arrived in the mail. For a while, his walls bristled with Post-it notes scrawled with quotes. Tommy stopped dropping around to see him as often. There wasn't much point. He was hardly ever home.

Then, two years ago, when Tommy's father started running his own trawler, heading out to sea in the blackness after midnight, Tommy and his dad moved in with Grandpa so Tommy wouldn't be alone before school.

What's going to happen to me now?

Tommy rubbed his forehead and shuffled out of the kitchen to the lounge, where his family stared at him, heads tipped to one side. Soft sounds like sticky toffee boiled over Aunty Shane's lips. All the tilted heads made Tommy feel seasick.

I'll never live with Aunty Shane and Bob and Mad and everyone. Over my dead body.

Tommy crossed his fingers.

That night, the wind tore at the cottage. It sucked in the windows, then spat them out, over and over again. The eucalyptus pelted bark against the bricks and scratched fingernails across the glass of Tommy's bedroom window.

Tommy dreamed he was trying to fix the outboard motor, but oil had made his hands slippery and the longer it took to fix, the more his father dissolved into the mist. He woke with his heart thudding.

Gulping for air, Tommy wrestled the damp bedclothes off his legs. The wind had died down, but the rain continued to fall in great grey sheets. It was as if the sea had turned upside down in the night and was tipping itself on the town. He pulled the blankets over his head.

That afternoon, with the rain and the wet clothes, the chapel was stuffy with so many people packed in around the walls. Tommy felt dizzy and glanced down at the paper shaking in his hands.

In loving memory
Dylan Tomas Evans
February 12 1975 – March 26 2007

The typing was fancy. Dad didn't like all that stuff. I could have told them that.

Tommy watched the photographs of his father flash up on the screen. He hadn't been able to speak in front of all these people. He stared at the slide show of his father's life.

Mum.

Tommy squinted, leaned forwards, and wished for the picture of his young, laughing parents to stay suspended for ever. Outside, he could hear more rain drumming on to the chapel roof. He shifted in his seat.

Last night, after dinner, Tommy had slipped away from his family's sympathy. In his room, he found Mad turning over books and toys.

When he tried to hide his diary, she asked what he was up to.

"Nothing much," he shrugged.

"Come on, Tom. I'll fight you for it." Her eyes bored into his.

"I'm writing a letter."

"Yeah?"

Tommy shook his head, blinked away tears. "About Dad."

In the following silence, Mad sat beside her cousin at his desk.

"I'll help."

Tommy felt his face flush. "I want to tell people about Dad, but I might forget things."

Mad nodded. She picked up a pen.

Tommy hadn't really cried until Mad stood up at the funeral, his letter pressed against her chest. When she began to read, Tommy watched her until his eyes ached.

"...My dad was a fisherman. We ate a lot of fish. Our best times were at sea – quiet, working, just whistling sometimes when we caught stuff. He was famous for his pizza and a tomato soup I didn't really like. He was good at climbing trees. He loved my mum, but she died. He taught me to sail when I was five. We nearly finished building our boat. It'll be better when I finish our boat."

Mad stopped reading. There was movement at the back of the chapel. A whisper began. Aunty Shane rubbed Tommy's back. Grandpa leaned across and smiled at him, but Tommy could see the edges of his mouth were twitching the wrong way. Tommy felt static charge the air as the mourners shifted from foot to foot.

The man from the funeral parlour was telling people to move their cars. Tommy looked around. The faces at the back blurred as people began to peel out into the storm. With the chapel doors open, the damp air crept under the seats and across the carpet. One of his father's favourite songs began to seep through the room. Tommy shivered.

Tommy stood on the steps of the chapel, squashed against the crowd of coats and legs. In the half-light, he could see a river of water rushing towards him, silver surges swallowing the plaques and gravestones.

He looked across to where his mother and his grandmother were buried in the Garden of Tranquillity. Posies floated past, their polystyrene holders tossed on the tide. A small pink teddy swerved in the current, waving a paw. Adults grabbed arms, gasped, their mouths dropping open at the flood gushing across the grass.

Tommy stepped out into the afternoon. The wind slapped at his face, bullets of rain exploded on his head. The storm ran off his new suit, and petals from the yellow rose in his buttonhole began to tear away and plop into the water.

Mud obscured Tommy's feet. He hopped forwards, splashing and landing with a thud on the soaked lawn of the cemetery. People clutched grannies and children to their sides; their coats spread out like black flowers as they disappeared across the flooded bridge.

The sprig of rosemary in Tommy's hand was a splinter, the purple flowers stripped away. He pulled back his arm and tried to skip it across the sudden lake, but the wind caught the twig and spun it back behind him, where it was lost in the churning mulch and earth from the cremation beds.

"Holy smoke." Mad's hair was plastered to her face and when she pushed it away, it stood in ridges on top of her head. She stared at the car park, where the vehicles were drowning, the tops of their roofs glinting in the deluge. "It looks like a car lake, a car graveyard. Come on, Tommy! Let's swim! I bet we could jump on the tops of all those cars to the other side." She grabbed his hand. She was shaking and laughing, guffaws snorting through her nose. "Oh man. It's freezing."

Tommy began to tremble. "I have to find Douglas." His heart thumped as he tried to wade back to the chapel, slower now the river was pulling against his knees.

Mad tugged at his jacket. "Douglas will be fine. He's at home, isn't he? Probably all tucked up with a revolting snack."

Tommy stared at her. "I brought him with me," he whispered.

Mad stomped ahead of him back up the lawn to the chapel. She splashed on to the verandah, and turned to wave. Tommy tried to run, to catch up, but he lost his footing. His legs buckled, and the fingers of the current held him down. He felt the air prickle out of his suit, the life pressed from his lungs. He drifted...

When Tommy began to fight for his life, there was water in his nose and he was weighed down, choking for air. He surfaced, coughed, kicked hard, began to retch. A figure shook aside the neck of his coat. Tommy realised he was on dry land.

"We've got a live one here, boys."

Tommy's grandfather bent down, whispered, "You gave us a real fright, lad. Two Evans men lost to a storm in one week wouldn't do at all, would it? Anyway, who am I going to share my quarters with if you leave me in the lurch?"

Tommy tried to sit up, but the weight of clothing made him struggle. Someone had taken off his suit and shirt and wrapped him in as many layers as possible.

Probably Aunty Shane.

"Grandpa," he managed, shivering. "I don't know where Douglas is. He was in my pocket."

His grandfather leaned down and loosened the first three coats. He then put one hand inside his own jacket, plucked out a tiny, bright-green thread and passed the baby snake over to Tommy.

"Yours, I think. I found him. He found me, actually – bit me on the finger. Probably just as well, what with the stampede out there. He would have been tree-python jelly by now."

"OK, Tommy?" Mad perched on the step beside him. She shook out her hair. "Your dad would have loved this, you know. Chance to get one of his boats out. He would have been rescuing people."

Tommy cleared his throat. "Yeah. Yeah, he would. He would have got out a kayak for sure." He paused. "Mad?"

"Yeah?"

"When you saw my dad, did you think he looked like he was asleep?"

Magdelene hunched her shoulders. "No."

"I didn't think so, either. I thought he just looked dead."

Tommy turned away. He thought about how

he would finish the boat, and how he would take Mad and his grandfather fishing.

Just before midnight, the floodwaters dropped and the people marooned in the chapel struggled out into the night. Tommy and his grandfather went home to the cottage, a tiny beacon of light above the sea. Tommy's grandfather ran a bath for him and made hot chocolate.

The old man raised his cup and sighed. "It'll be OK." He patted Tommy's hand. "Us orphans have to look after each other," he said.

Tommy nodded. His grandfather looked very old.

That night, Tommy lay on his side and stared at Douglas in his terrarium. His eyes stung. He sat up and blew his nose hard into a tissue.

If I can finish the boat, then I can think about Dad.

The storm pounded the cottage. Branches lay twisted across roads, power lines danced in the gusts and flame-tree flowers glistened like blood on the sodden earth.

Dancing lights woke Tommy in the early hours of the morning as they pulsed across the bay. The wind roared and he could see the straining silhouettes of the she-oaks outside his window. His heart began to hammer.

No! *The boat*! Sandpiper!

Tommy scrambled through the house, grabbing a torch and his father's coat from its peg by the back door. Two 4WDs were in the car park above the beach, their lights trained on the boats at the jetty. Down at the water's edge, figures were retying mooring ropes and shouting to each other whenever there was a lull in the wind's scream.

Tommy pelted down the bush track and across the seagrass above the dunes, sinking into holes the storm had drilled into the earth. He turned his torch in the direction of *Sandpiper*'s mooring.

Can't see.

He rubbed his eyes, stumbled down on to the beach, threw his torch beam again at the boat.

Nothing.

The wind was freezing and the salt spray was stinging his eyes. Tommy bent forwards and scuttled to the rocks below the jetty.

Nothing.

He dropped to the sand and sat in the lee of the wind with his back against the rocks.

Sandpiper *has slipped her moorings and left me behind*.

Tommy didn't want to look again. He slumped in the dark and rubbed his head.

If I hadn't argued with Dad, he wouldn't have gone out by himself.

"Come back!" Tommy shouted. "Please come back," he whispered.

Just before first light, the storm had wrung itself out and the sea was still and sullen. Tommy stretched and peered over the rocks. *Sandpiper* was gone, her mooring rope torn and floating from the post. He cast his torch beam one last time out to sea. Then, as he was turning away, he caught a glint of gold near Breakneck.

Sandpiper!

Tommy was sure his boat was out there, waiting for him. He launched the old dinghy from under the jetty and ripped the engine into life. He caught his boat just as she began to roll out to sea. Balancing his weight, he tied a rope around *Sandpiper*'s tattered hull and began to haul her in. As Tommy steered closer to shore, a figure on the beach shone a torch to guide him home.

He heard his father's voice in his head, "Bring her in, Tommy. Steady mate. You know what you're doing. That's it. You can do it. Good on you, Tom."

Grandpa waded into the ocean to help. He spoke softly and Tommy strained to hear what he was saying.

"Don't ever do that again, son. You're just like your father, but you don't know everything yet."

"I'm ten years old, Grandpa. I had to get her back. Anyway, you and Dad helped me."

The old man turned away. The sun was streaking across the sea.

"Let's have a big breakfast, Tommy. My shout."

The bush was waking up as they started up the track. A pair of black cockatoos cut across the green. The birds called to each other as they went, shrieking their way above the rainforest.

Their dusky wings flapped in long, stiff movements, and their red tail feathers were ostentatious in the dawn. Tommy and his grandfather stood still for a few moments, then, arms linked, began their climb home. At the top of the headland, Tommy glanced back to where *Sandpiper* was moored. In the new day, the sea winked and sparkled.

"The storm's put me back, but I'll get her finished, Grandpa."

The old man stood, catching his breath. He threw an arm around Tommy's shoulder.

"Give an old fella a bit of a push up this last bit, son."

Later, when his grandfather was in the kitchen, Tommy slipped down to the beach.

I'm sorry, Dad. Sandpiper's a bit bashed about, but I know what to do. It's not too bad. And you know that gold paint? I reckon it's OK. I'm learning to love it.

Tommy pushed his cap off his forehead. *She'd be seaworthy in a week. She had to be.* He wanted to take Grandpa and Mad out at Easter.

Grandpa arrived in the afternoon with a basket of scones and a flask of sweet tea.

"I have a proposition for you," he said.

Tommy grunted.

"A plan."

Tommy stopped.

"I'll help you here and in return you help me with the cooking and a bit of tidying up. We'll have to work harder without your dad, but we'll be a good team. Sometimes you can go and stay at Aunty Shane's place." He paused. "Only if you want. No need for any big changes, though."

"I don't..." Tommy's voice wavered. He started again. "It's just..."

His grandfather pulled him in close. "I know, son. You've got every right to be scared. I am, too."

Tommy hiccupped, burying his face in his grandfather's sweater.

"But we have this boat to fix," Grandpa growled.

Tommy pushed him away. "You don't know anything about boats."

"Ah, well. That's where you're wrong, lad."

"But Dad always said..."

"Yes, well, that's as maybe, but I happened to complete a certificate in catamaran design from the University of the Third Age last year. I'm sure we'll be able to muddle through."

Tommy laughed; a small, tickling bubble that hurt his stomach as it burned out of him. The old man was picking through the tool box. "Are we doing this, or what?"

That night, strangers came to the cottage; wide, weathered men with checked shirts and bellies tucked into jeans. When Grandpa introduced them, one cuffed Tommy under the chin, the oldest slid a punch off one shoulder, while the other two stared at him, shaking their heads. All of them told Tommy he was a "chip off the old block".

Tommy could smell the sea and the oil from the trawlers on them as they moved through the hall to the lounge. Grandpa fished out the brandy from the sideboard and sent Tommy to bed. Through the wall, Tommy heard the rise and fall of conversation. He had seen the Costas on their boats and at their shop in Flame Tree Bay. His father had always nodded to them before glancing around and whispering something like, "Respect, Tommy. Remember that. Those old Italian-Australians have saltwater running through their veins."

The visitors became louder as the hours ticked by but, always, above the din, Tommy could hear his grandfather.

The next week was cold and rain sheeted down for two days in a row, but Tommy spent every spare minute he could fixing up *Sandpiper*. Finally, he was done.

Easter Sunday was bright, but Tommy could see from his window a breeze was beginning to whip up the surface of the sea and clouds were gathering. At the kitchen table, he found a note.

Tommy,
Had to go to town. Meet you at Sandpiper at 8 am.
Grandpa
P.S. Bring coat - looks like rain.

Tommy fed a mouse to Douglas, then slipped him into his backpack. When he got to the beach, Mad was leaping about, making the boat lurch from side to side. Tommy stood with his fists clenched.

His cousin leaned over the side, then jumped into the surf. "What's the matter, Tom? Looks like you've seen a ghost."

Grandpa's head popped out of the cabin. "Aye, aye, cap'n. Welcome aboard!"

Tommy glared at his cousin. "Grandpa, I thought... I wanted to be the first aboard... to launch her."

"And so you will be. Of course! After all your work. We were just tidying up." He gestured to the boat. "She's all yours."

Mad and the old man stood to attention, saluting as Tommy clambered past. The cedar cabin was glowing with polish and the sharp, sappy scent of the wood smelled clean and promising. In the corner, something gleamed. Tommy gasped: it was a terrarium for Douglas.

They launched *Sandpiper* with a bottle of lemonade bubbled over her bow. Mad suggested Tommy rename the boat for his father, but

Tommy shook his head. Curlew sandpipers were clever and fast and liked to forage in deep water along the shore. They stuck together and wheeled through the sky in clouds of brothers, sisters, cousins, uncles, aunts, mothers, fathers and grandparents. He liked that.

"Let's have a look at the blessing of the fleet before we go fishing, son."

Tommy hesitated. Every Easter, for the Festival of the Sea, the Italian fishing families brought a priest from the city to bless their boats for the next year. Anything seaworthy was allowed.

"I dunno, Grandpa. It'll be jam-packed. All the boats in town will be on the water."

"*Sandpiper* will be in her element then, won't she?"

When they turned past the stone breakwater into the harbour, the boats seemed to part, forming a corridor to the main wharf. Tommy's heart thudded. With the wind in the riggings and the music and the crowds, it was difficult to hear the announcements from shore. Boats jostled bows and a catamaran scraped *Sandpiper's* side. Tommy grabbed the wheel.

"Stop, Tommy! Stop!" his grandfather bellowed. "It's OK. She's supposed to earn her battle scars."

The old man's hands were steady next to Tommy's on the wheel, and they turned her nose out to sea. The crowd behind them cheered. The crews blew whistles and trumpets and, everywhere, streamers rippled through the blue air. Tommy stared at his grandfather.

"You're leading the blessing of the fleet, lad. Remember the Costa brothers visiting? They asked specially. Said it would be an honour. 'Specially for you and your dad." He coughed. "Go on, Tommy. Lead them out."

Tommy's grandfather stood back. He wiped the wind from his eyes with a tissue. They had faced death and here was hope again. He didn't need a Post-it note for that.

Sandpiper flew through the water. Tommy made room for his grandfather at the wheel and scrambled out of his coat.

There was no sign of rain.

About the Authors

Jo Nadin
is a former broadcast journalist and Special Adviser to the Prime Minister. She has written several books for younger readers, including *Jake Jellicoe and the Dread Pirate Redbeard* – a *Blue Peter* book of the month and Lauren Child's pick of the year on Radio 4's *Open Book* – and *Maisie Morris and the Whopping Lies*, winner of the Lancashire Fantastic Book Award. She is also author of the acclaimed **Rachel Riley** series for teenagers. She lives in Bath with her daughter.

Karen Ball
is the author of *Starring Me As Third Donkey*, published by Puffin. She has also written two non-fiction titles on Pompeii and Leonardo

da Vinci for Usborne Children's Books. Her next project is contributing to a series of books called *Sisters of the Sword*, about samurai girl warriors in 13th-century Japan.

Linda Newbery
writes fiction for young readers of all ages. Her young-adult novel *Set in Stone* was the Costa Children's Book of the Year 2006 (formerly the Whitbread Prize); *The Shell House* and *Sisterland*, also for young adults, were both shortlisted for the Carnegie Medal. Novels for younger children include *Catcall*, *Nevermore* and *Andie's Moon*. Linda is a regular speaker at schools, libraries and festivals, has judged the Whitbread and Guardian awards, and tutors workshops for writers of all ages for various organisations including the Arvon Foundation.

Many years ago, **Helen Williams** sailed from England on a banana boat to take up a teaching post in rural Jamaica. She fell in love with the island and its people, and made it her home. Now retired, she writes stories about Jamaican children. Her fantasy story for young adults,

Delroy in the Marog Kingdom, will be published by Macmillan Caribbean in 2008 under her pen name, Billy Elm.

Tim Wynne-Jones

has written over two-dozen books including novels, picture books and three collections of short stories. He has twice won the Canadian Governor General's Award for children's literature for *Some of the Kinder Planets* and *The Maestro*. The latter, retitled *The Survival Game* was short listed for the Guardian Children's Prize. So was his mystery, *Boy in the Burning House*. His latest is *Rex Zero, King of Nothing*, sequel to *Rex Zero and the End of the World*, which was published last year to great acclaim in both Canada and the United States.

Journalist **Kim Kitson** is a former teacher (biscuit packer, gas-meter reader and the school canteen's worst mathematician) and has lived in New Zealand, England, Wales and Australia. She has had a story for adults published and another broadcast on national radio in Australia. 'After the Storm' is Kim's second story for younger readers. Her MA thesis in children's literature and literacy was based on representation of 'the other' and the extraordinary lives of 'ordinary' people continue to inspire her. Kim is working on a story about the 'big dry' in Australia and is planning her first novel about a girl's search for her mother.